LIVING THE DREAM

JOELY TONNA

© Joely Tonna

First edition November 2018

Cover design by Hope Evie Jepson

For Tèa x

CHAPTER 1

Bertie Brownlee flew just high enough over the evergreen trees to avoid snagging her school uniform. Circling above the school, she watched her classmates below brave the icy December chill as they shuffled in shivering lines across the playground towards the hall. Letting out an excitable "Woohoo!!" to attract their attention she dive bombed so close to their heads that her broad angel wings skimmed their hair.

"Bertie Brownlee, stop this nonsense!" screamed Mrs Bland, angrily. Bertie ignored the teacher's demand and swooped skywards, preparing for another dive bomb, this time aiming for Mrs Bland.

"Bertie Brownlee!" came her teacher's furious cry. Bertie caught the laughter of her classmates on the up-wind as she prepared her rapid drop towards Mrs Bland's thatch of wild, woolly grey hair. This was bound to impress everyone. Down, down she flew, wings stretched wide, the air whistling through her perfect white feathers, then…

THWACK! She was knocked to the ground like a skittle.

"Oooowwwwwww!"

"Bertie Brownlee, stop this daydreaming RIGHT NOW! You are meant to be walking to the hall – it's really not that difficult." The teacher's booming voice brought Bertie crashing back to reality. "If you insist on standing there staring into space like a zombie it's no surprise that you got mown down by the year 1 class.

Now get up and move it! You will *not* ruin this nativity!" Mrs Bland helped the pile-up of 6 year-olds scattered across the frozen ground as Bertie heaved herself up and dusted down her angel costume. Her cheeks flamed with shame and, despite the freezing temperature, she felt her skin prick with sweat. How could she not have noticed thirty children dressed as stable animals bumbling towards her? Maybe it really was time to stop the daydreaming. If only she knew how.

As she made her way into the hall, she was fully aware of her classmates sniggering behind her. But that was a regular thing. She was used to that. What worried her was the thought of Mrs Bland cutting her solo from the nativity. She had threatened to do so after the episode with the red paint and the new white skirt. That hadn't really been Bertie's fault. She had only drifted off for a few seconds thinking about spells for teachers and, ok, she should've been *painting* with the brush and not waving it around fully loaded like a magic wand, but Mrs Bland should've been looking where she was going. Anyway, white is a ridiculous colour for anyone to wear at school.

The assembly hall was full to the brim with excited mums, dads and camera wielding grandparents all rubbernecking to see their little darlings in their nativity costumes.

The children shuffled and squeezed into their places on the floor either side of the stage and Bertie took her spot among the large group of startled

Reception children. She gazed across at her Year 6 class dressed as kings in regal crowns and matching ruby velvet gowns. They looked so cool, so bonded, so disconnected from her. And there she was feeling like an awkward giant who'd just arrived in munchkin land. 'She's not an academic child,' her teachers had told her parents at any given opportunity, 'so we'll do our best to nurture her talents where we can. It's the daydreaming you see, it hinders her development.' So here she was with her talents well and truly nurtured, about to sing a solo; a massive great angel surrounded by tiny people disguised as stars wrapped in far too much tinsel with the cute factor turned up to 11.

Despite the humiliation, Bertie wasn't going to complain. Her classmates hated the nativity, saying it was for little kids and they were probably right, but Bertie loved it as it meant she could indulge in her one huge passion...CHRISTMAS! This was the thing that she thought about every single day of her life, all year round. Even in the height of summer she yearned for those cold, frosty days where the sun stayed hidden allowing the fairy lights on the Christmas tree to twinkle from morning 'til night; those days when you could snuggle on the sofa under blankets, when the candles would dance and flicker and the glitter would shimmer and sparkle. She applauded those shops that stocked Christmas cards, crackers and decorations in September as they made the magical season last that little bit longer. The thought of Christmas tickled her tummy and sparked a smile to her lips. It was what got her through the tedious school days and the many, many embarrassing moments that she experienced on a regular basis. It was a time when she felt safe. Finally, it had all come around again and she could hardly contain her excitement.

"Thank you all for coming along today." The head teacher's voice swept a hush across the hall. His dreary tones were fatal for sending Bertie off into another daydream but he was thanking her mum for painting the stunning Bethlehem backdrop for the play and Bertie busily craned her neck to spot her in the audience. 'Mum really should paint again,' she thought as she waved at her blushing mother. 'She's just so gifted.'

She looked to the left and right of her mum and noticed that someone was missing. "Where's Dad?" she mouthed, but her mum just shrugged and mouthed back, "I don't know, sorry." He'd been so excited about hearing Bertie sing that she was surprised by his absence. Despite every teacher telling him what a lost cause his daughter was and how worried he and his wife should be about her lack of focus, Bertie's dad always told her how incredibly proud she made him. 'Don't listen to those dinosaurs,' he'd say. 'What do they know about real life? All they care about is teaching you maths that you'll never use. At least when you daydream you dream big. That's a gift. If daydreaming was on the national curriculum you'd be skipping Secondary school and heading straight to University.' He really was the best dad she could wish for.

She started thinking about the time the family went for a roast dinner at the local pub and how he'd insisted they wore clothes her mum had made for the dressing up box. He'd chosen to wear the ballet tutu, which was far too small for him and a large proportion had disappeared up his bottom. She remembered spraying a mouthful of drink everywhere when he'd tried to do spins and stretches at the bar with a totally straight face. That was the thing with him; people were never sure whether it was ok to laugh. It made Bertie all the more proud to have a naturally funny dad who really didn't care what people thought of him. Like the time he rode her tiny pink Barbie bike all the way home from school. The stuffy mums hadn't seen the funny side, especially when he twanged the tinny bell and rode right through the middle of their snobby huddle. She'd laughed so hard at their horrified reactions her stomach had ached the next day.

"Albertine, stop laughing. Albertine! Albertine Brownlee!" For the second time that morning, Mrs Bland's hissing voice pierced her thoughts and broke her daydream. "For goodness sake child, who are you laughing at?! Get on that stage!" Bertie should've been embarrassed but instead she threw Mrs Bland an angry glare. No one uses her full name, not even her parents. Mrs Bland threw back a far angrier look, which read, 'you ruin this show and I'll take you down.'

Bertie clambered to her feet and led the tiny, tinsel clad tots onto the stage for their moment in the spotlight. She'd been so immersed in her daydream, she hadn't even noticed that the show had started and the narrators had already led the audience part way through the greatest story ever told.

She took centre stage with the tinsel tots spreading out around her, each intently seeking their spot on which to stand. The audience cooed at their cuteness, hardly noticing Bertie at all. Eventually silence fell. The baby Jesus in a manger was carefully placed at her feet and the lights dimmed. Suddenly all eyes shifted focus towards her. She looked so serene, so majestic, so angelic; her long curly blonde hair cascading around her shoulders, big wide eyes framed by long dark lashes. Her bejewelled costume, cleverly hand-crafted by her mum, shot splintered rainbow rays darting in every direction as it shone under the bright, solitary light. Even Mrs Bland smiled on in awe. Bertie stood still with hands held in prayer, her eyes staring straight out across the crowd. She may have appeared calm but she was so nervous she was sure the people in the front row could hear her heart beating.

No one made a sound. They all waited.

Then she began to sing.

There was no music, no backing track, just her beautiful pure, clear, liquid gold voice. Her soaring pitch perfect voice expressed every word of the song with such passion that she took the audience with her on her daydream of the stable with the baby Jesus in Bethlehem. For a moment she *was* that angel who had brought the good news to the shepherds and who watched over the newborn king. And, for a moment, the audience believed her.

As she held the last note of the song there was silence. She opened her eyes with a start, suddenly realising where she was. The audience leapt to their feet as a roar of cheers and applause filled the hall. The clapping and cheering grew louder and louder and Bertie was completely stunned by their reaction. She noticed quite a number of the women were wiping away tears, her mother among them. Was this really happening? Reality seemed to have merged with one of her daydreams of an outstanding TV talent show audition, leaving her confused and bewildered. Mrs Bland caught her eye with another glare, reminding her of how she'd been screamed at during rehearsals for being dozy and missing her queue to leave, so she quickly ran off to make way for the kings and their camels.

As the nativity came to an end and the audience left the hall, there was only one topic of conversation.

"Wasn't that angel incredible?"

"Who was that girl with the voice of an angel?"

"That angel should be on the West End stage, she's amazing. Who *is* she?"

Nobody could quite believe the talent of one little girl who had blown them away. Did she know, they wondered, just how good she was? But back in the classroom things were rather different.

"Who does Bertie think she is, some West End star?"

11

"She was really showing off."

"Why was everyone cheering, she wasn't that great."

Bertie heard every word her classmates had said. She assumed she was meant to. She was so ashamed that she took her clothes and got changed in the toilets where she could cry in private. Never before had she wanted her dad so badly. Why wasn't he there to hear her sing?

She couldn't possibly have known then that her dad, the man she adored so greatly, was about to shatter her Christmas dream.

CHAPTER 2

Only Bertie's headless body could be seen from the living room that evening. She had poked her face through the curtains and was gazing longingly up at the star-filled sky, thinking about the events of the earlier nativity. The words of the cruel girls played on a constant loop in her mind, stinging with every repeat. She shook her head in an attempt to rid her mind of the negative thoughts and forced happy festive ones in their place.

"I'd give anything for a white Christmas," she sighed.

Her mum sat sewing beside her. "I hate to say this but we don't get much snow this far south, Darling."

"Well maybe it'll be different this year and we'll get a healthy dumping of the white stuff on Christmas Eve, just like in the films."

"Yes, Sweetie, and maybe Santa will pop in for a glass of sherry and we can all roast chestnuts on the open fire – that we don't have."

"Santa's coming round for tea! Santa's coming round for tea!" All too often, Mrs Brownlee forgot how sarcasm was completely lost on a four year old and she now had to deal with her son Billy running laps around the living room in uncontainable excitement.

"Wouldn't that be amazing," Bertie whispered, staring obliviously at the stars. "And then a choir would turn up at our house holding lanterns and singing carols in perfect harmony and all the neighbours would spill out into the street and perform a perfectly choreographed dance routine."

"Oh Bertie," her mum smiled, catching Billy by his belt loops. "Even I'd like that dream to come true."

"You see! My world of dreams is far better than the real one we all live in. Anyway, what are you making?" Bertie's head reappeared in the room and she swung round to check out her mum's handiwork.

"It's a surprise for your dad."

"Is it a costume for Christmas Day? Do I have one?" She leant forward for a closer inspection of the fabric but her mum quickly whipped it away.

"Yes and yes," came the clipped reply. "But, no prying or peaking, you know it ruins it if you guess what it's going to be." Bertie realised the project was in its early stages and it was therefore far too soon to predict it's outcome.

Just then she heard a key in the door. She leapt over the back of the sofa and dashed across the living room to greet her dad. He'd know what to say to make her forget all about the mean girls; he always did. He'd sent an apologetic text blaming work for his absence at the Nativity earlier but she was over it already. It was his last day of work tomorrow and she couldn't wait for him to finally relax at home with the family and play all of those silly parlour games and eat the rubbish food that Mum only allowed them to have at Christmas. He always made this time of year so incredibly magical. A rush of excitement fizzed in her stomach and a little squeal of delight escaped. But, by the time she reached the door, her excitement was cruelly dashed. Something was very wrong.

Mr Brownlee usually came crashing into the house, whistling or singing. He'd always throw his coat and bag in the general direction of the coat pegs, ruffle Barry The Dog's fur, squeeze his children too tightly, and bounce in, sighing with relief that his dull day at the IT office was thankfully over.

But not today.

Today he came in quietly, hung his coat and bag carefully on the peg, ignored Barry, pecked Bertie limply on the cheek and padded into the kitchen mumbling a quiet "Hi". This wasn't like him at all. Mild panic filled her mind like frozen fog. She'd never seen him like this before and she didn't know how to react. What could possibly be wrong? What should she do? Should she say something? Maybe if she acted naturally he'd be fine. He was probably just shattered.

"Dad, Mum says we can make a gingerbread house tonight. Billy and me have been waiting for you to get home 'cause you're so good at cutting out all of the pieces. I've dug out that Christmas CD so we can have a songfest. What do you think?"

He didn't respond. Instead he ushered everyone over, sat them down at the kitchen table, hung his head and, in a low voice, made an announcement. There was no warning, he just came out with it.

"Head office are sending me to work on a project in London and I'm afraid it means that…I won't be here for Christmas." Bertie gasped in horror and the blood drained from her face. Had he really said what she thought he'd said?

"What do you mean you won't be here for Christmas?!" she shrieked. "You finish work tomorrow. Of course you'll be here, Dad!"

He flicked her a glance and placed a reassuring hand over hers, casting his eyes downwards. He'd dreaded telling Bertie more than his wife as he knew how devastated she would be. It broke his heart knowing that he would be responsible for ruining this precious time for his family.

"I'm so sorry, Bertie, I know it's all very sudden but there's nothing I can do about it. The company I work for took over a massive job today from some other IT firm, which pulled out at the last minute. It's a huge building refurbishment and it has to be ready for a big business re-launch by the first week of January. My boss says that unless we want to lose our jobs, we have to go."

Bertie's eyes brimmed with tears and her breath caught in her throat. She couldn't believe what she was hearing. Surely she had misunderstood him. Surely there'd been some mistake. London? That was absolutely miles away. She tried to speak but nothing came out.

"Look, the good news is that the boss has put me in charge which means the money is fantastic and he's promised me a large cash bonus too." He was trying in vain to convince both himself and his family that this was a positive thing but they all knew it was a lie. He'd already been told that he'd be working ridiculously long hours, six days a week with only Christmas Day off – there was nothing positive about any of that.

A silence hung in the air like a black cloud. He looked to his wife for some sort of response.

"Darling, I'm so sorry, that's absolutely awful - for all of us," said Mrs Brownlee, softly. "I can't believe this is happening and at this time of year too. But if there's nothing you can do about it then of course you must do what you need to do to keep your job. We understand don't we, Bertie?"

How could she possibly be this understanding? Did she not know what was happening here? Bertie could feel the desperation rising inside of her.

"How can they just spring this on you at the last minute and expect you to say yes, Dad? It's not fair, you should say you're not going."

Mr Brownlee forced a smile. "Unfortunately, Mr Hardwick is a heartless bulldog who'll sack me without hesitation if I say no. I know it's utterly hideous and I can't bear the thought of being apart from you guys but what can I do? At least the extra money will come in handy. You know how we've been struggling lately."

Bertie couldn't argue with this. She knew how he hated having to deny them any treats because they couldn't afford it and they hadn't had a holiday since Billy was born. She sighed loudly, and covered her face with her hands.

"Oh!" she squealed, with sudden wide-eyed excitement. "How about we all come and stay in London with you? We can rent somewhere over Christmas!"

She felt sure her light bulb moment had solved the problem but her dad shook his head slowly.

"I'm going to be staying with Uncle Andrew and his flat is tiny. I'll have to sleep on the sofa so there certainly wouldn't be room for us all. The job is in a very wealthy area called Richmond and it'd be far too expensive to rent anywhere there, especially over Christmas.

"Look, maybe with the bonus we can afford to go away somewhere special next summer. How about that?"

"Yay! Somewhere with a swimming pool, Daddy?!" cried Billy. He was such a summer lover but then, he was the total opposite to Bertie in almost every way. She wondered if he even understood what it meant not to have Dad around for Christmas. Who would take them 'carol busking' or ice-skating or to the reindeer farm? Who would decorate Mum's Christmas cake really badly on Christmas Eve and who would eat all of the orange crèmes and those hard toffees that nearly pulled your teeth out? *And* who would run around the house at the stroke of midnight on New Year's Eve dressed in nothing but a kilt singing Old Lang Syne while the neighbours cheered? These were Dad's traditions.

Bertie's dream of another perfect family Christmas had been completely shattered. Her beloved dad wouldn't be around for the most important time of the year and she didn't think she could bear it. It was as though her life had come to a screeching halt. Her special Christmas - the season she thought about all year round - the time of year she loved even more than her birthday and which defined her whole world - had been cancelled.

Then the tears fell.

CHAPTER 3

That night, Mr and Mrs Brownlee stood outside their daughter's bedroom door listening to her sobs. They debated whether to go in to comfort her and talk things through once more but decided instead that she needed to try and sleep. They knew she understood that her dad wouldn't go away unless it was absolutely out of his control and they also knew she didn't hold it against him, but this didn't stop them feeling her pain.

When Bertie finally fell asleep on a tear soaked pillow, she had a dream.

All around her was dark. A haunting sky hosted ghostly clouds blown fast and furiously by a fierce howling wind. The light of a full moon revealed a road ahead, which she was to travel. She knew not where it would lead. Nonetheless she set out, soon discovering the road was on a hill, which grew steeper with every step she took. Her legs felt as though they were made of concrete and she struggled to heave one foot in front of the other. Heroically, she battled against the raging wind, the steep hill and the weight of her legs. As she did so, she became aware of faceless people zooming past her and dashing up the hill with effortless ease. One after another, they whizzed past, coldly taunting her, carelessly knocking her out of their path to the mysterious destination ahead. Then, as one person overtook, he paused, seemingly concerned. He stopped just long enough to inform Bertie that her dad was at the top of the hill then shot off. Sensing something was wrong she knew she had to find her dad. He needed her help. She used every muscle in her tired, heavy body to drag herself to the top of the impossible hill to reach the father she loved so dearly. On and on she trudged, the muscles in her legs burning like fire, the cruel wind biting at her cheeks until finally she reached the summit. She lay at the top panting with exhaustion only to discover she was too late. Her dad was gone. But where? Desperately, she grabbed people and pleaded with them to tell her where she could find him but no one knew and worse still, nobody cared. An overbearing feeling of failure and great loss engulfed her as she lay weeping on the cold, hard ground, her heart shattered into a thousand tiny pieces.

Suddenly, appearing beside her was the same shadowy figure she had spoken to on the hill. He knelt down and whispered in her ear.

"*Don't lose him again. Keep him close.*"

Bertie woke with a start, sitting bolt upright in bed. Her hands felt the soft duvet around her and it took a few disorientated moments before realising that the events hadn't actually taken place. Immense relief washed over her and she flopped back onto her bed. What an intense dream! She lay there analysing it for some time and, as sinister and distressing as it was, it had somehow put things into perspective. There was no way she could be parted from her dad and there was no way she was going to let him go to London without his family. *She* was going to take action.

CHAPTER 4

It was usual practice for Mrs Brownlee to drag her reluctant daughter to school in the mornings, especially on the last day of term, but the next day, Bertie had surprised her mother with a request to leave early. With last night's dream still vivid in her mind, she simply had to be with her dad over Christmas so, if her parents weren't going to bother trying to find them somewhere to stay in London, she would do it herself.

With only ten minutes before the school bell would ring, she dashed straight into the IT suite when she arrived, turned on a computer and entered her personal login. As soon as the Internet fired up she logged onto a search engine, entered 'houses for short term let – Richmond, London' into the search bar and hit return. Just how expensive can it be to borrow a house for a few weeks?

Within seconds, her eyes were greeted by a glorious list of the most stunning houses she'd ever seen. As she scrolled excitedly through the array of shiny wooden floored living rooms and glossy cream coloured kitchens she imagined herself decorating a Christmas tree in these magnificent homes. She gasped at their beauty and gasped again when she clocked the shocking prices beside the pictures. Holy Moly! The rent per week was more than her dad earned in a year.

Realising that the search had thrown up the most expensive properties first, she felt a sudden surge of hope and quickly scrolled to the end of the list to the more affordable ones. But her heart sank when she saw what was on offer - a pokey little one bedroom flat above a (presumable stinky) fish shop and a studio flat which even Barry The Dog would turn his nose up at. Not wanting to be defeated she tried search after search of areas close to Richmond but each seemed as expensive as the next. Why did he have to go and work in one of the most desirable areas in London?

Whilst searching, Bertie noticed an advertisement for an estate agent by the name of 'Stead and Kemp', which repeatedly flashed up on the screen desperately advertising its properties for rent. Having exhausted all other options, she decided she had nothing to lose and clicked onto their website. In order to search their properties on offer, she had to enter some details, but when it came to entering the amount she was looking to pay per week, the website made a rude rejection noise followed by a notice informing her that 'there were no properties available at this price'. Bertie was half expecting another notice saying 'how dare you insult us by entering your details, you clearly are not worthy.'

She slumped into the swivel chair and groaned loudly. It seemed that her great idea was not so great after all. How could she have been so stupid as to assume she'd be able to resolve this situation by herself just because of her stupid dream? She was way out of her depth here. As she was about to close down the computer and heave her sorry butt outside to sulk in the playground, she heard a 'ping!' She had received an e-mail from Stead and Kemp Estate Agents. Expecting it to just be a registration acknowledgement, she half-heartedly double clicked but to her surprise, the e-mail displayed a letter in a rather fancy font. It read:

Dear Miss Brownlee

Thank you for registering with Stead and Kemp estate agents.

We see from your details that you are seeking to rent a house in the Richmond area and it so happens that a suitable property has just become available.

The owner of the property, a gentleman by the name of Mr Muse, will be away over the Christmas period and does not wish to leave his beloved home unoccupied. He is, therefore, looking for someone to take care of his house during his absence. This would mean a short term let of two weeks commencing Sunday 20th December to Sunday 3rd January.

It is Mr Muse's decision to offer the house to you and your family for the ridiculously low rent of £100 per week. This, I am sure you will agree, is an incredibly good deal and, I might add, one which we would not usually encourage.

The house has 4 large double bedrooms, lounge, kitchen, dining room, games/music room and conservatory. To the rear of the property is an extensive garden and an outbuilding housing a heated swimming pool and Jacuzzi.

It is in the picturesque area of Barnes, which I'm sure you will find to your liking. There is a beautiful village pond, traditional English pubs, wine bars, convenience stores, quaint shops and wonderful places to eat. The river Thames is just a stones throw from the property and the fabulous river pathways are perfect for long dog walks.

Please find attached some photos for your perusal. If you and your family are interested, please contact me as a matter of urgency. Mr Muse is very keen to find occupants as soon as possible.

Very best regards,
Mr Kemp

"Oh. My. Word!" she whispered. Her mouth hung open, her eyes were as wide as saucers. This house was on a far grander scale than any that she'd seen on the websites. She scanned photo after photo of bright, spacious, inviting rooms full of plush modern furnishings, luxurious cream carpets, big bouncy beds, all topped off with state of the art décor and gadgets. The huge living room had two enormous shimmering chandeliers suspended from the ceiling and the most beautifully ornate fireplace with space beside it for a very substantial Christmas tree. The swimming pool was of rock star standard and the games room had everything from a full size table tennis table to guitars and a baby grand piano. Bertie could not take it all in. She leapt out of her swivel chair and victory-danced her way around the desks, punching the air and squealing with delight. Her prayers had been answered with a miracle!

Celebratory dance complete and excitement calmed, she sat back down to reply to the e-mail. But it was then that she began to feel a little uneasy. Something didn't quite add up. She had only just registered with the agency and this e-mail had come through almost instantly. Would estate agents be open so early? And who on earth types a letter that quickly? What was going on? Was this someone's idea of a joke? Mild panic set in as it dawned on her that she hadn't really thought this through. She couldn't possibly tell her mum and dad about this house anyway, as they were sure to tell her off for entering their details into websites without their permission. Should she call the telephone number to check it out? But what would she say? What's more, what would the estate agents say when they found out Miss Brownlee was an eleven year old girl? Then again, could she let this opportunity slip through her fingers? That's if it was real of course.

The sound of the school bell gave her a start. She closed down the computer and dashed off to class, only to spend the entire day dreaming about the house and how wonderful it would be to spend Christmas in the lap of luxury.

Luck was on her side for once as Mrs Bland was nowhere to be seen. Apparently she'd been signed off until further notice for 'severe stress'. Bertie wasn't sure what that meant but she didn't care as in her place was a wonderfully warm and friendly supply teacher, who didn't seem to mind Bertie's day dreaming one bit. In fact, she seemed strangely interested in it and asked her odd questions about the sort of dreams she had. With no actual schoolwork to be done on the last day of term, the two of them had time to chat about their best dreams and how no one understood a daydreamer. It was a good excuse for Bertie to keep well out of the way of the spiteful girls in her class and it was the perfect way to end a dreadful year at school. Secretly, and a little guiltily, she prayed that severe stress was a very long-term illness.

When she got home that afternoon, she drove herself mad going round and round in circles about whether to tell her parents about the amazing house. After much agonizing, she decided to stop dwelling on it, and anyway, it probably wasn't available anymore. A house like that for such cheap rent would've been snapped up in an instant.

As she huddled together with her family on the sofa after tea, she had finally pushed all thoughts of beautiful houses with swimming pools and games rooms far from her mind and just enjoyed the cosy moment. But that magical moment was short lived as it was rudely interrupted by the home telephone ringing. Mr Brownlee was nominated by his family as the lucky person to answer the call and he reluctantly grumbled off to the study. A few minutes later, Bertie heard him call out to her mum.

"Bea, come here quick!!" His voice was urgent and screechy. Mrs Brownlee rushed into the office after him.

"What is it, Love?"

"You'll never guess what's happened. Our daughter - she's a total genius!" He was grinning insanely.

"What's happened, what have I done?" Bertie called out as she scrambled off the sofa, her heart pounding in her chest.

"Well," began Dad, breathing deeply to calm himself, "I've just taken a call from an estate agent in London who said a 'Miss Brownlee' had contacted their website. They've found us the most amazing place to stay in London!"

Bertie's face burned with fear as her dad proceeded to explain all about Mr Muse and his magnificent house in Barnes to his wife. He was almost breathless with excitement.

"Brian, Brian, slow down! What are you saying, that some random guy wants to offer us his house for next to nothing? Isn't that a bit odd? And what, Bertie, were you doing putting our details on the Internet?! You know you shouldn't do things like that!"

Just how much trouble was she in? "I only wanted us to be together for Christmas," she protested. "I didn't actually think anything like this would happen."

"Bea, can't you see, this is incredible!" soothed Mr Brownlee. "Our daughter has used her initiative and achieved something that neither you or I had thought of. She's solved a problem and found a way for us to be together. Plus, a very kind hearted gentleman who is full of Christmas cheer has shown generosity and selflessness by offering his home for stupid money. Never underestimate the spirit of human kindness, my darling wife. Plus he's probably horribly rich and doesn't need the cash. Check out these photos that he's e-mailed me. We *have* to stay here."

After examining the photos of the chandeliers and the rock star pool, Mrs Brownlee was not only sold on the idea but screeching as much as her husband.

Bertie should have been as excited as her parents; after all, this is what she had wanted. Instead she was still totally perplexed. Just how did someone type that e-mail so instantly that morning? And why would this Mr Muse, a man they didn't know, offer such generosity to her family? Plus, what were the chances of this house in

29

this location being available for the precise number of days that her family had required, for a ridiculously low rent that they could afford? It all seemed too much of a coincidence; besides, good things like this just didn't happen to her family. And it was that night that Bertie had one of her recurring dreams.

She was being chased by…well she couldn't tell who it was, but they were coming after her and she was desperate to escape them. She was struggling with all her might to sprint as fast as she could but, frustratingly, she was running in slow motion and her feet weren't making contact with the ground. The tired muscles in her legs were like jelly as she tried with all her might to force them down to the grass beneath her but the most her feet could do was pathetically scrape the ground. She was going nowhere. Every time she looked behind, the chasers were getting closer, their anger intensifying. She was panting and panicking and sweating. She tried to scream out "Help! Someone help! They're going to get me," but no sound would emerge. Again she tried to run with all the energy she could muster, desperately forcing her body to move forward but still she was going nowhere. The dream usually ended there with no explanation and no resolution but this time something changed. This time the chasers suddenly vanished. Gone.

Just like the night before, Bertie awoke, panting and sweating to an intense feeling of relief. How happy she was that the chasers didn't catch her. And how glad she was that she wasn't that rubbish at running in real life.

Before long she drifted back into a peaceful, dreamless sleep.

CHAPTER 5

"Oh, isn't this a gorgeous place, Brian? It's like a little village. Who'd have thought London could be so beautiful!" Bertie studied her mum's enchanted expression as they arrived in Barnes on the frosty Sunday morning and an anxious knot in her stomach twisted and tightened. The journey had been so long, she'd had far too much time to stew over all of the possible outcomes of this trip. What if she was about to let her family down; what if there really was no dream house in Barnes? What if they'd been led on an elaborate goose chase by a wicked prankster out to gain some sort of sick satisfaction from other people's misery? Or, what if it was some kind of trap and they were all going be murdered in their beds by thieves and robbers?

'You have arrived at your destination,' announced the posh lady on the Sat Nav as they pulled up a crunchy gravel drive. It led to a very tall, very grand, brown-bricked house with bright, white trims and a glossy mint green door.

"Wow!" breathed Mum as she craned her neck to take in the magnificence of the building. "It's incredible."

Bertie felt sick. She couldn't even look as her dad climbed out of the car and strode up the deep stone steps of the house in case her worse fears were realised. Mr Brownlee pressed the bell and waited for what seemed like an eternity while nothing happened.

No one answered the door. He looked over at his family and shrugged his shoulders.

"Ring it again," mouthed Mum from the inside the car. Her excitement hadn't waned one bit, which only heightened Bertie's anxiety. Her stomach had now twisted into a double knot with a bow and she slipped low down in her seat burying her head in her hands. The agony was too much. She couldn't bear the thought of having to leave her dad at Uncle Andrew's tiny flat and spend Christmas without him. It would simply tear her apart. The fight to hold the tears back caused an agonising ache in her throat. She swallowed hard.

"Ah! You must be Mr Brownlee!" came a sudden shrill voice. "I'm Mr Muse. It's so wonderful to meet you!"

Bertie gasped, filling her lungs with air for what seemed like the first time in hours. She couldn't even attempt to hide the audible "yes!" and accompanying air-punch that followed. Mr Muse was real! That meant his house was real and his rock star pool was real and his games room and the chandeliers and the Christmas fireplace were all real. The twisted knot and sick feeling dissolved into a tingle of excitement. The nightmare had just become a wonderful dream. No wild goose chase and no elaborate hoax, just a fabulous, fabulous house.

"Come in! Come in!" shrilled Mr Muse, gesturing madly to Mrs Brownlee and her children in the car, "It's freezing out here. Come in and warm up."

Bertie unclipped her seatbelt, her hands fumbling with eager anticipation. She craned her neck to get a good look at Mr Muse and her exhilaration switched to utter disbelief.

"What on earth is he wearing?"

"Shhh," hushed her mum. "He could be in women's underwear for all I care, he's letting us stay in his house for next to nothing."

Bertie couldn't take her eyes off this strange man as she clambered out of the car and crunched her way up the gravel to the door. She'd somehow imagined him to be an older gentleman, slightly stuffy – the sort who still wore a pressed shirt and smart trousers despite having long since retired from his important job in the city. Instead stood a much younger man dressed in a slim-fitting gangster style three-piece pinstripe suit with a white shirt and fat, black tie. He wore bold silver cufflinks and had a pocket watch chain hanging from his waistcoat. His look was set off by scruffy, once-white Converse trainers and a mop of blonde shaggy hair that looked like it had a phobia of hairbrushes. This all made him very difficult to compute. Was he a surfer dude off to a fancy dress party dressed as a Mafia boss? Or perhaps he was a rebellious rich kid who had a habit of blowing his inheritance on lavish houses and crazy clothes? And what was with that voice?

Bertie could tell that her dad was having trouble pitching his approach to this unusual character as his faded Scottish accent had ramped up to full-on Glaswegian. It was a nervous thing.

"Let me introduce everyone," he announced as his family joined him on the doorstep. "Och, now this is my wife Bea, my daughter Bertie, my wee son Billy and please, call me Brian. Oh and that noise in the car is Barry The Dog. Everyone, this is Mr Muse, the very kind gentleman whose fine house this is."

"How lovely to meet you all!" shrilled Mr Muse again as he greeted each of them with the enthusiasm and warmth of a long lost relative. Then without warning he gathered them all in for an unexpected, and rather over-familiar, group hug. "It's just so wonderful to have you all here!" he cried. "This is a beautiful moment!" Bertie was completely baffled. She knew it was rude but she couldn't stop staring at him. He seemed to be three or four different people morphed into one rather strange being. Quite unlike anyone she'd ever come across before. Fabulous house – extremely strange owner.

"And Bertie, thank you for finding us, this is all down to you," he announced.

"Us?" She hadn't even considered the possibility of him having a family.

"Yes, me and my house. We're a bit of a double act," he replied with a chuckle.

"Oh," she breathed, in bewilderment. But before she could make any sense of this peculiar statement, he had swept everyone up from the freezing doorstep and ushered them into the house.

Inside, it was warm and wonderfully inviting. A distinctly familiar smell of Christmas hit Bertie's nostrils, causing a timely distraction. It was emanating from somewhere down the hall and while the rest of her family hung up their coats and exchanged pleasantries with the odd host, Bertie snuck off to follow the alluring, spicy scent.

Down the hall she trotted where she came upon a set of floor to ceiling glossy white double doors. She grabbed the huge gold handles and pulled the doors open. Suddenly, her eyes were met with a glorious sight, for it was here that Bertie found herself in Christmas heaven. She stood wonderstruck in awe of its beauty. Had Mr Muse walked into a top London store and bought the whole Christmas display? (Bertie wasn't allowed to visit big stores at Christmas after the time she decided she wanted to live in the Christmas department of Harrods and refused to leave).

Delicate fairy lights wove their way neatly through boughs of holly adorning the deep, wide windowsills that framed the room. Little stripy stockings, obviously knitted by Elves, hung expectantly from the ornate fireplace and, along the mantelpiece, more fairy lights danced among sprigs of mistletoe and scatterings of deep red frosted berries. The flickering radiance of a host of candles around the hearth gave a warming glow that highlighted every touch of Christmas magic this opulent room had on offer.

And just as she had dreamed, next to the crackling fire stood a magnificent Christmas tree so tall that it scraped the high ceiling. It was adorned in a symphony of purple and silver baubles, stars, feathers, angels and snowflakes all hanging in wondrous harmony. Realistic little candles sat proudly at the end of every other branch, lighting the tree with a festive golden glow and, taking her regal place at the very top, was the prettiest fairy with the finest silver hair, antique lace dress and diamond encrusted wand. Her painted face beamed with pride for all that lay beneath her and rightly so as this really was quite the most magnificent tree Bertie had ever seen.

At the foot of the tree lay exquisitely wrapped presents, far too perfect to be ripped open. It crossed Bertie's mind that perhaps this wonderful Mr Muse (no longer strange and odd) had bought them all a little gift but she quickly dismissed the idea, deciding instead they were probably just for decorative purposes only, although what he would've chosen for them was a fabulous mystery to ponder.

"I'm so glad you are staying here, I know my house will really like you." Bertie swung round to find Mr Muse standing beside her, smiling down with mesmeric eyes.

"What do you mean, your house will like me?" she asked, trying desperately to smile through her bemusement. She hoped her knee-jerk response hadn't sounded too rude.

"Well, it's very important that a house likes its occupants," he chirped back, seemingly oblivious to any rudeness, intended or otherwise. "A house can be a very magical place with the right people in it you know, especially if you're a dreamer like you. But you'll find out more about that later I hope." Before Bertie could ask what on earth he was talking about, he had danced off into the hallway to find the rest of her family.

"Come on, come on everyone, follow me and I'll show you around the rest of the house. I must get going before the light fades." Bertie stood in a bewildered silence. He really is an odd man, she thought. Generous, but odd. Fancy calling her a dreamer when he'd only just met her.

Mrs Brownlee was already in the kitchen when they came in. She had fallen in love with the cream units, modern appliances and under floor heating. She was found with her face planted on the work surface and her arms stretched out either side sighing the words 'real granite.' Mr Brownlee calmly attempted to prize his wife away before Mr Muse thought better of renting his house to a bunch of nut jobs.

Every room in the house seemed to hug them as they entered. Their feet sank into thick luxurious carpets and squishy sofas took away their worries and woes. The light smell of Christmas and happiness throughout the house made the family feel they'd lived here their entire lives.

"I want you to enjoy this house as if it were your own," insisted Mr Muse. "Don't worry about anything getting damaged or dirty, just love the house and it will love you back". There he goes again, thought Bertie, talking about this house as if it were a real person.

"What, even the cream carpets?" laughed Mrs Brownlee. "I don't think we'll let Barry into the house as they wouldn't be cream for long!"

"No, no! Please do let him in, Mrs Brownlee, it really doesn't matter, it'll be fine. I want you *all* to enjoy this house; you really mustn't worry about a thing. It'll all be taken care of. Now! On to the bedrooms!" The Brownlee's raised their eyebrows at each other and followed as he swept off up the stairs and into yet more rooms on the seemingly never-ending tour of this magnificent house.

"This is the room that I've chosen for you, Bertie." Mr Muse swung open the door and stood back, ushering the family in. They were surprised to find the bedroom was considerably larger than their living room at home. Bertie bounced on the enormous bed and snuggled in the giant marshmallowly duvet. She knew then that she never wanted to leave this house.

"Check out the view, Bert," said Dad, peering through the heavy golden drapes. "Beats the view of the neighbour's shed from your room back home!" Bertie bounced off the bed to join him and stared in wonder at a stunning pond edged with pretty willow trees set in the heart of the village. She spied Canadian geese and a variety of other wild birds sharing the space with people who had come to drink in the tranquil beauty.

"This is so lovely. And so *You.*" Bertie turned around to see her mum standing next to a small, ornate wrought iron fireplace with fairy lights around it and a Christmas tree decorated exquisitely in reds and golds. She'd been so taken by the marshmallow bed, she hadn't even noticed it when she'd walked it.

"Yes, I had a feeling you'd appreciate the colour scheme, Bertie," said Mr Muse. "I took a chance on it."

"They're my favourite Christmas colours," she cooed. "It's perfect. All of this is just perfect." However odd she found Mr Muse, she really admired his impeccable taste. He clearly knew his stuff when it came to interior design, to Christmas decorations and to choosing amazing houses in beautiful locations and this made her question whether his fashion sense really was way off the mark or whether he knew something that the rest of society was yet to catch on to.

As soon as the sun began to fade, Mr Muse gathered his things in a sudden rush to leave. "Goodbye everyone. Got to dash," he trilled. "Enjoy this lovely home. Relax, swim, take it easy and sleep as much as you can. The beds here are to die for!" But before the Brownlees had time to thank him properly for his kindness, he'd danced off down the drive in a flurry of arm waving and a sing-song "goodbye, goodbye, enjoy, enjoy!!"

Once gone, the family closed the door and stared at one another in a stunned silence. Then....

"Arrrhhhh! We're so lucky!" shrieked Mr Brownlee, bouncing up and down.

"Wooohoooo! I can't believe it!" screamed Mrs Brownlee running round in circles.

"Yeeeessssss! I love this house!" shouted Bertie, following her mum.

"I can make as much mess as I liiiiiiiike!!!" yelled Billy, punching the air.

"No you caaaaaaan't," his family chorused.

CHAPTER 6

Their first evening in the Dream House was spent dashing around excitedly, exploring each of the rooms in more detail.

"Now *this* is my favourite room," announced Dad as they all piled into the games room. Looking around at the vast array of musical instruments on offer he suddenly stopped in his tracks. "Oh my word, a Fender Stratocaster!"

The much-coveted electric guitar was identical to the one he used to play years ago when he was in a band. He promptly plugged in and turned the amp up to 'very loud'. Much to the utter horror of his daughter, he then proceeded to prance around the room like a rock star.

"Oh, no, no Dad! Don't dance! Don't do that dance! It's so embarrassing," Bertie screamed, batting him away with her arms, but he just carried on. She looked over to her mum for support, only to find her practically hugging a baby grand piano.

"Oh my, you are so beautiful. Come to mummy," she sighed as she stretched her arms over the piano, laying her face on the keys.

"Oh my goodness," Bertie groaned, shaking her head in shame. "Please tell me I'm adopted." Her parents failed to hear her due to the racket Billy was making with a tambourine. Bertie took hold of a microphone and plugged it into an amp.

"Right!" she yelled, causing a squeal of feedback. "No more noise!" Her family all jumped at once and stared at her. "Dad, you are not Jimi Hendrix. Mum, stop kissing the piano and Billy, *gently* on the tambourine or you'll give us all tinnitus. Why don't we actually play something that makes a pretty sound?"

"Ok, Ok," agreed Dad, laying off the strings for a moment. "Let's play one of my songs then. Seeing as it's Christmas, how about 'Santa's Wish'?"

"Oh yay!" screamed Billy and they all laughed as he chanted the lyrics "Santa won't come if you don't - go - to - bed!!" They joined in with their instruments and sang at the tops of their voices laughing hysterically at their punk version of a song Mr Brownlee had written as a lullaby for his young children.

"Right," he sighed, hanging up the guitar. "I really must go to bed now otherwise I won't get up in the morning."

"I wish you didn't have to work tomorrow and could just hang out with us here all day, Dad, we haven't had this much fun together for ages."

"I know, Sweetheart, so do I," he sighed, bear hugging his daughter. "But at least I'll get to see you guys when I come home from work now. I know it'll be really late but Mum and I have decided that you can both stay up until I get in. That way we'll get to spend some time together."

"Do you like your job, Daddy?" asked Billy.

"That's a bit random!" said Dad, a little taken by surprise.

"Do you?" Billy asked again. Mr Brownlee hesitated. He had no idea what made Billy ask such a question and for some reason it caught him off guard. He hesitated for a little too long before answering.

"N…yeah…yes it's fine, Billy. It's not going to change the world or save lives but it's a job and it pays the bills." Bertie noticed a sudden drop in her dad's tone of voice. He seemed sorrowful. Lost. Then just as suddenly, he sprang back to life again.

"Come on, you two, off to bed; Santa's watching. He'll be making that naughty and nice list, now off you go!"

Bertie did as she was asked. She kissed everyone goodnight and made her way upstairs to unpack her things and get ready for bed. But as she cleaned her teeth, her dad's words resonated in her head and she was left with a nagging feeling that all was not well. She'd never really thought about whether or not he was happy at work. He went off cheerfully enough every day and if he'd complained, she certainly hadn't been aware of it. Even the excitement of the Dream House and her luxurious new bedroom couldn't take her mind off things and she lay awake worrying about him for some time. But she couldn't compete with the heavenly powers of the marshmallow bed and eventually she was sound asleep.

That was when everything changed.

CHAPTER 7

Within seconds of falling asleep, Bertie was dreaming that she was in a completely white, never-ending space. It wasn't a room as there were no walls or windows and it wasn't outside as there was no grass or sky. It was just perfectly pure white infinity. She was suspended in nothingness. To her delight she could make her weightless body turn somersaults and spins with the agility of an Olympic gymnast and she giggled as she twisted, turned, hung upside down and spun on her head until she was dizzy. When she tired of this she floated on her back with her hands supporting her head and heaved a contended sigh. It was sheer bliss.

After a short while though, the novelty of zero gravity began to wear thin and it was at this moment that something dawned on her.

She was awake.

Sometimes you have dreams where you're convinced you're awake, but you are in fact dreaming. But Bertie was actually conscious.

"I can't be awake," she said aloud, giving her left arm a large pinch. "Ouch! Oh no! I can feel that and I'm pretty sure you don't feel pain in your dreams. Oh my goodness what's happening? Where am I?"

Then panic set in.

"Oh my goodness!" she shrieked in alarm. "I'm dead! I'm dead! I must be dead because surely this is heaven isn't it? All this white nothingness is heaven! Oh no! OH NO!

I'm dead!

I'M DEAD!

How did I not know that I'm dead?

Hang on - How did I die?" She looked down at her body and her heart sank.

"Oh no, I'm in my PJs. I'm in heaven - in my PJs! Oh my goodness."

"Ah, Bertie you're here already."

The disembodied voice gave Bertie an almighty start. She squealed in alarm and spun around to see who it belonged to but there was no one there.

"My dearest, darling girl you are not dead," came the voice again.

"God? Is that you?" she whispered, desperately searching all around.

"No, no, I'm not God," laughed the voice, "although, without wanting to blow my own trumpet, some people have said that I'm a lot like him."

Out of the nothingness, a small black dot suddenly appeared before her. It wriggled at first then danced above her head before hovering a few feet in front of her face. She watched in astonishment as it began to spin wildly round, growing bigger and bigger, taller and longer before popping out into a man-shape. A pinstriped man shape with a head of very messy blonde hair.

"Mr Muse! It's you! What on earth is going on? What are *you* doing here?"

"I live here," he chuckled, wafting around her. She shook her head and blinked hard.

"But this isn't Barnes, what happened to Barnes? Where is *here*?" she demanded in exasperation. "This is all too surreal. Am I dreaming? If I'm not dead and this isn't heaven, I must be dreaming right? I really don't think I like this dream. I want to wake up!" She began thrashing herself around like a landed fish in the hope that she'd suddenly wake in her bed but the only thing she managed to do was look very silly.

"Dear girl," he soothed, "I can assure you that you are *not* dead and this is definitely not heaven. Sweet child, welcome to Dream World."

"What? Dream World?" she repeated. "Dream World?" she repeated again. "What is Dream World a...a...a...and how exactly did I get here? More's the point, *where* is it?"

"Please, Bertie, don't be frightened, this is a beautiful place, well, it will be once you've made it your own." He raised his hand and gestured to the whiteness that surrounded them.

"Made *what* my own? What are you talking about?" Would anything this man said ever make any sense?

He gave Bertie a broad smile and stopped floating long enough to place a reassuring hand on her shoulder. "Dream World is the place where dreams happen."

"Dreams? Dreams happen here?"

"Yes. Bet you weren't expecting to find yourself here when you went to sleep tonight?" Bertie just glared at him. She wasn't amused and she wasn't buying into this nonsense either. This was definitely a dream. Of course it was. She knew she was being rude but this wasn't real life so it really didn't matter what she did or said. And what a weird dream this was. She decided she might as well go along with things to see just how obscure it could become. She really hoped she remembered it in the morning.

"So what happens then? How do you make the dreams?"

His answer was delivered with such conviction it was almost believable. "Well, first of all we start by seeing into the dreams that occur naturally and analysing them, then we set about sorting them out."

"You can see into peoples dreams? Really? Why do you do that?" she asked; her disdain was beginning to give way to genuine interest.

"To help people on earth. That's our job here in Dream World you see. If we notice that people need help, we analyse their dreams to try and make sense of what is going wrong. Then, if we think it's necessary, we become part of their dreams and feed them messages to influence them in order to change the course of events in their lives. It is our aim to sort out their problems."

"Right," Bertie said in stunned wonder. Fixing people's lives through their dreams without their conscious awareness, if only this was real it would be awesome.

"We also spend a great deal of our time creating dreams from scratch," he continued. "They're the best ones. That's when we can really get to work." Bertie noted the mischievous glint in his eyes and started to feel she was getting sucked into this totally unbelievable situation in which she'd found herself.

"So…you get into peoples dreams?"

Mr Muse nodded.

"And you make dreams for people too?"

"Yup."

"You actually *live* inside their dreams?"

"For a short while."

"But I had no idea any of this went on!"

"Good!" he laughed. "You're not supposed to know, otherwise we wouldn't be doing our jobs properly. But it's not always an easy task, which is why us Dream Dwellers need help - hence your arrival here. I was rather hoping you'd assist us."

"Dream Dwellers?" She questioned. "I'm sorry, this is all a bit too much to take in."

"My apologies," he said, realising his haste. "Dream Dwellers are people who come to work in Dream World. I am a Dream Dweller."

"But you live in the lovely house in Barnes that we're renting from you." She shook her head as if this would bring her to her senses. "Look, this is one of my weird dreams. I'll wake up in a minute and it'll be time for breakfast." She tried floating away from him and this silly dream, immediately realising she had nowhere to go.

"It's not time for breakfast yet, we haven't even got started. Now, first of all I need to explain about the house." He floated to catch her up. "I live there some of the time but my real home is here. You see, that house is a portal and it allows people with the gift of extreme dreaming, like you, to travel here to Dream World and do the work of a Dream Dweller. I feel that you are ready for this now, Bertie. That's why I made sure your family came to stay."

"I *knew* there was something odd about that whole 'cheap house' thing," she said narrowing her eyes. "So you arranged that?"

"Yes I did. I'm sorry if it caused you any kind of distress but I had to make sure you made it here. Like I said, I think you're ready."

"Ready for what?" She was finding it a little tricky keeping up.

"You're different, Bertie. Your dreams and daydreams are unlike most peoples. You don't just dream, you *experience* that dream. For you, it's not a case of drifting off, you go in deep. It's no wonder you've found maintaining focus at school so impossible. There are very few people like us you know. You're special. You, Bertie, possess the ability to help others."

For the first time since she'd arrived in Dream World, she was silent. She *was* different, she knew that because her daydreaming had caused her so much grief over the years and it would be a huge relief to regard it as a gift rather than a burden. But helping other people by getting into their dreams? Really? She couldn't help remain doubtful as she observed her surroundings once more.

"So, where are all the dreams then? I can only see white."

"Ah yes," he said following her gaze. "I can see why you'd be more than a little confused. Come with me. It's probably better if I show you around first, then it'll all become very clear."

CHAPTER 8

"You've always wanted to fly haven't you? Remember that daydream you had the other day about dive-bombing Mrs Bland's dodgy hair? That was a classic."

Bertie was gobsmacked. "How do you know about that, Mr Muse?"

"Well, I'm your Dream Dweller. I see all your dreams and daydreams, that's my job. Right, time to fly. Follow me." Without warning, Mr Muse took off and started circling above Bertie's head.

"Where are you going?" she called.

"To see some friends of mine. Come on, there's so much I need to show you."

"And I fly, how exactly?"

"You just do," he shrugged. "Have a go, you can do it."

Bertie launched herself forward, flapping her legs as though she was swimming and before she knew it, she was up along side Mr Muse, soaring through the air like a migrating bird.

"Woohooooo! This is way better than any flying dream I've ever had."

"Are you having fun?" he called across to her, his mop of blonde hair flapping madly in the breeze.

"Oh yes! This is the best fun I've had in ages." She flew higher and higher before diving down like a hungry seagull plunging the sea in search of fish. For a moment, she stopped worrying about where she was and whether or not this was a strange dream and instead, savoured the moment.

They had been flying a short time when she noticed splashes of colour appearing on the horizon.

"What's that up ahead?"

"Oh, we're nearly there. This is what I wanted to show you, Bertie. You're going to enjoy this. Follow me."

As they flew on, the white emptiness that had surrounded them gradually blended into the brightest blue sky. Glancing down, Bertie realised that the splashes of colour she had seen was in fact a beautiful garden full of the most magnificently vibrant flowers. They swooped down to get a better look and the sweetest floral scents filled the air. Every type of flower from the tiny Forget-Me-Not to the exotic Bird of Paradise danced in the gentle breeze, boastfully aware of their majesty. In the middle of the field sat a quaint white cottage with roses around the door and a delightful garden pond. As they drew closer, the front door swung open and a pretty young woman appeared. She was dressed in a long floaty, floral summer dress and she wore a delicate daisy chain around her head, which hung down the back of her long, silky dark hair.

"Hello, Mr Muse," called the young woman. "It's lovely to see you again."

"Stella! It's lovely to see you too," cheered Mr Muse as he landed skilfully next to her. "I wanted to introduce you to your new neighbour. This is Bertie." He gestured over to Bertie who made a far from skilful landing straight into the lady's garden furniture.

"Oh! Oh, are you OK?" Stella gasped, dashing to Bertie's aid. "Is this your first time in Dream World?"

"How did you guess?" Bertie laughed as she clambered to her feet, her cheeks stained with embarrassment. Flying was one thing but landing was a whole other set of skills.

"Well, it's very nice to meet you," smiled Stella, sweetly.

"It's very nice to meet you too," Bertie flustered as she dusted herself down. "This is such a beautiful garden, it must have taken you ages to plant all of these flowers."

Stella shot Mr Muse a look and raised her eyebrows.

"Oh, I haven't quite explained everything yet," he said.

"I see," smiled Stella, "well then allow me." She turned her garden chairs upright and they all sat down in the sun-lit garden.

"Well, Bertie, this is my Dream Zone, D-Zone for short. Everyone in Dream World has one. It's our own space and we fill it however we wish. On earth I hate being miserable and cold during the winter months so I've created the perfect home in the country where every day is springtime. I could never find a place like this on earth but when I became a Dream Dweller, I had the chance to make my dream a reality here in Dream World."

Bertie looked to Mr Muse. "Is that why it was all white when I arrived? Was that my blank D-zone?"

"Spot on, Bert. What you thought was heaven was in fact your space to do with as you desire."

"Do you like the sound of that?" Stella asked excitedly. "The best thing is, you get to choose anything you want, even if it's not possible on earth. Do you know it never rains here – it's sunny every day and I never have to water my flowers."

"Wow, that does sound pretty cool," Bertie cooed. "Could I make it snow every day?"

"If you wish," replied Stella, a little surprised. "It doesn't even have to be cold if you don't want it to be."

"Oooh, warm snow! Fantastic!" Bertie's eyes widened with delight.

"I'm afraid this is a flying visit, sorry Stella," Mr Muse cut in. "We must be leaving now as I have lots more to show Bertie before she wakes up."

"No problem, it was really lovely to see you both. And, Bertie, whenever you return here and you need some help or just someone to chat to, you know where I am. Here, take this." Stella bent down to pluck a tiny bright pink flower from her garden and placed it in Bertie's pyjama pocket. "You'll need that in the morning."

"Oh, thank you so much," Bertie said politely, wondering what on earth the significance was of this seemingly kind gesture.

The pair waved goodbye to Stella and her beautiful flower garden as they took off once again.

"She's lovely," Bertie called across as they made their ascent.

"Very lovely, and one of my best Dream Dwellers too. She started young like you and she's helped a great number of people. Ahhh...look over there in the distance, isn't this great?" Mr Muse was pointing up ahead to their next destination. The green meadow and its vibrant flowers gradually merged into an aqua marine sea beneath them. A beach with fine, white sand stretched out as far as the eye could see and alone on the shore sat a large wooden beach house. It was a finely crafted construction boasting a long veranda with steps sweeping down to the shore.

There on the veranda, swinging on a hammock, lay a well-built man in rolled-up shorts, tatty faded T-shirt and a battered old pair of flip-flops. He sang a catchy little tune to himself while shading from the blinding sun.

"Hey! Curtis! I didn't think we'd find you here at this time!" cried Mr Muse, landing on the decking.

The man obviously wasn't expecting company and was taken by surprise. As he lifted up his sunglasses to see who had disturbed his rest, he lost his balance and tumbled out of his hammock, landing in a heavy heap on the floor. He clambered to his feet and trotted ungainly over to Mr Muse with his arms outstretched.

"Hey man! What bring you 'ere? I not seen you for a while ya'know!" He threw his arms around Mr Muse and the two men laughed raucously as they man-hugged.

"You're usually on earth whenever I come by, Curtis. It's good to see you. Are those dreamers of yours keeping you busy?"

55

"They are man, they are ya know. Soooo busy. I'm havin' a lickle rest now before I go back home. How you been man? You good?"

"I'm great thank you, really great. Curtis, may I introduce you to my friend Bertie. This is her first time here and I'm just showing her around so that she can get a feel for the D-zones and meet some of her new neighbours."

Curtis held out his hand. "It's nice to meet you, little lady," he said as he bent his large frame down to greet her. She stared up at his huge smiley face, heavily lined by too much sun and years of laughter. He lifted his sunglasses to reveal eyes the colour of the ocean.

"Hello, it's very nice to meet you too," she said in a small voice, all too aware of her fleecy pyjamas on such a hot beach.

"So, what you think of me D-zone? You like it 'ere?"

"I love it, it's very peaceful."

"Peaceful!" he screamed, "Peaceful! Me dreamers never give me any peace, girl!" and he roared with laughter once again. Bertie laughed too. She'd never met someone with such a big character before. He was most fascinating.

"May I ask why you chose the sea?"

"Well now, I'm from Jamaica but we 'ad to leave for America when I was a young man. I missed da beaches ya know. Missed dem, missed dem." He sighed and shook his head. "I used to dream of paddling in the sea, catchin' fishes…" He drifted off in a moment of blissful memories. "…and now I can come back when I like to *my* beach - to get some peace!" He threw his head back and belly laughed once again.

"You mustn't let the dreamers take over. You work too hard." Mr Muse gave Curtis a friendly slap on the back. "I'll let you get your rest and enjoy your D-zone,"

"Ahhh no!" cried Curtis, "You can't leave them for long or they won't get the 'elp. Mine need the 'elp."

"Well, they are certainly in good hands with you, my friend," smiled Mr Muse. "I'm terribly sorry but we've got to dash. I'm sure we'll see you again soon."

"Goodbye, Curtis, pleasure to meet you," Bertie called as she flew off.

"Goodbye, little lady. And make sure your D-zone is peaceful!"

They could still hear Curtis' roaring laughter as they took to the sky leaving the white sandy beach and the turquoise sea in their wake.

Once airborne they glided gently for a while so they could chat. "I wanted you to meet Stella and Curtis as they are your closest neighbours and two of my more experienced Dream Dwellers. They come most nights you see, although Curtis lives on the other side of the world to you so is on a different time zone. That's why I was surprised to see him here now. He must be having a nap or something."

"Oh right, so Dream Dwellers still live on earth then? I got the impression they lived here all the time."

"No, no, they're just regular people with normal every day lives, so they can't be here all the time. Once a person with the special gift has proved they can make it as a Dream Dweller they are awarded a portal house on earth. This enables them to travel here to Dream World in their sleeping hours and continue their vital work. Now you're going to ask me why my house in Barnes is so grand aren't you?" he laughed.

"Well, yes it had crossed my mind actually." She was glad he'd brought it up as she'd have thought it far too rude to ask.

"The greater your achievements here in Dream World, the higher the reward on earth. Let's just say I've been around a long time." Bertie could tell he was being modest and sensed she was in the company of a very accomplished Dream Dweller. "Most people only come here when they are needed, which can be the odd day here and there or every day for months on end. It depends on who needs help and what the problem is. If they're not needed for ages they can still come and spend time in their D-zone to relax during their earth sleeping hours."

Mr Muse turned so that he was gliding along on his back as though floating in the sea. Bertie copied him. She thought for a moment.

"Aren't you tired when you wake up the next day? Will I be tired tomorrow?"

"Not at all. We never feel tired. In fact, most Dream Dwellers say they feel extremely refreshed after a night in Dream World."

"So am I not in my bed anymore then? I mean if my parents came into my room would I be gone?"

"Good question," he said, raising his index finger in the air. "Your body is still in your bed but your mind and spirit are here. I always say the most important bits come to Dream World. You don't need your physical body because you recreate it when you arrive. You could create a totally different one too if you wanted."

"How do you mean?"

"Well, we quite often have to change our physical appearance in dreams that we create, otherwise dreamers would wonder why they keep dreaming about the same person. Watch this." Bertie looked on as Mr Muse turned and floated upright then morphed into a wizened old man hunched over a walking stick before quickly morphing back.

"Wow!" she whispered, "that's awesome."

"Anyway, come on, enough of this chit-chat, I want to whizz you past a few more D-zones. We won't have time to stop, there's too much to do but I want you to see a little more of Dream World before our time is up." He flew off at high speed with Bertie in hot pursuit. She really couldn't get enough of all this flying. Surely it could never get boring.

As they soared through the air, she was in total awe of the breath-taking sights beneath her. A patchwork of never-ending D-zones networked across this magical new world, their contents expressing the untamed imagination of their Dream Dwellers' minds. Some had chosen oceans with inflatable houses that bobbed happily on the gentle waves while others chose to live in mud huts in lush emerald landscapes with wild lions and antelope as their harmonious neighbours. There were large tents perched on the side of snow-topped mountains and there were regular houses in regular streets. She saw castles with moats, tacky modern mansions, twee little cottages, winding rivers, the dessert, the rain forests, the pine forests, the lakes, the green hills, the bright lights of cities with casinos and bars and the peace of the countryside with fairies and elves. Some chose dinosaurs as pets while others grew fields of candyfloss. Bertie even saw mermaids splashing in someone's heart shaped swimming pool and, by far her favourite, was an enchanted garden inhabited by a family of rainbow coloured Unicorns. Everything was here, every D-zone blending effortlessly into the next, every person living in their dream home.

Some time later they found themselves back in the wide-open whiteness where they'd begun.

"Those people had such amazing D-zones. Is there any limit to what they can choose?" Bertie asked, slightly breathless from all the flying.

"Not really," shrugged Mr Muse. "Anything is possible and it can be changed as often as you like. If you got bored with green rolling hills you could create a luxury villa by the sea if you so desired."

"I know exactly how I want this place to look." Bertie closed her eyes and day dreamed of the perfect house. "When can I start to create my own D-zone?"

"You already have, my child. Open your eyes."

She spun around to see soft snow tumbling silently over a beautiful Tudor cottage on a lantern lit, cobbled street. Beside it sat quaint little toyshops and old fashioned tearooms. Outside the cottage stood a proud Christmas tree covered in exquisite decorations that winked and sparkled and, wandering around the large snow covered garden that surrounded the house, were miniature reindeer.

"There it is!" she gasped. "That's my house! That's my perfect Christmas house! And it's twilight too, my favourite time of day." She approached one of the reindeer and stroked it lovingly between its antlers. "Don't worry, I won't give you a red nose," she whispered. "That wouldn't be fair."

"So what do you think of Dream World now, Bertie? Do you still think this is all a dream?"

She shrugged her shoulders. "Oh, I don't know, Mr Muse. Maybe I won't know what I make of all this until I wake up tomorrow. Whatever it is, it's absolutely wonderful and I love my little house. There is one thing that I'm not too happy about though."

"Oh?" said Mr Muse, raising his eyebrows.

"It's just that, I feel a bit silly in this amazing place wearing my pyjamas."

"Ha ha! Oh my! Yes I totally forgot to arrange that, I'm so sorry." He was relieved that her dissatisfaction was easily corrected.

"Just close your eyes and think of an outfit that you would like to wear when you're here."

Bertie did as she was asked and when she opened her eyes again, she looked down to see she was wearing a beautiful deep red velvet coat with a white fur collar. Underneath was a stylish (yet practical) black satin jumpsuit and on her feet were spectacularly sparkly black ballet shoes.

"That's more like it," said Mr Muse approvingly. "A perfect choice, Miss Bertie, and very festive indeed."

"Thank you so much and thank you for my gorgeous house!" She squealed with delight and ran off towards it. Slowly, she turned the handle of the heavy wooden door and pushed it open to reveal a warm and inviting living room with the desired fireplace, comfy old furniture and, of course, full on Christmas decorations throughout. "Now I really could invite Santa round for a glass of sherry and some toasted marshmallows."

CHAPTER 9

Snow had covered the D-zone Tudor cottage like a cotton wool roof. Bertie stepped out of the house and picked her way across the soft white garden to find Mr Muse sat beside a small statue of a winged man set on a pedestal.

"This is lovely."

"It's pretty cool isn't it? A thing of beauty and great power," Mr Muse whispered with reverence.

"I don't remember requesting a statue though," Bertie said plonking herself down next to him in the warm, dry snow. "Come to think of it, I saw a lot of these in the D-zones. Who's this dude with the wings?"

"Ahhh he is very important," said Mr Muse in hushed tones. "He is our God here in Dream World."

Dammit! She'd called their God 'Dude'. How disrespectful. She blushed and thought about trying to back-peddle but knew from experience that it always made things worse. She gazed admiringly at the sculpture instead and prayed Mr Muse wasn't offended by her inappropriate choice of vocabulary.

"This is Morpheus, the Son of Sleep - God of Dreams," he explained. "Morpheus was the first person to send messages through dreams. He could also take on any form he desired so that he could appear in dreams in different guises. These statues are a gift to us from Morpheus; they are his legacy."

"Wow, a gift from a God. This is all a bit too much, I'm really not sure I'm worthy," said Bertie, shuffling with embarrassment. "I've only just got here and I've been given so much."

"But Bertie, Morpheus wanted us to have these statues. Without them we cannot continue his work."

"Really? How come?"

"Because it's through these statues that we see the dreams."

"You see dreams through a statue?" She wondered how on earth such a thing could be possible.

"Look, I'll show you. Are you ready?"

"I think so," she replied, not really knowing what she should be ready for.

"OK. Stand up."

Bertie got to her feet, dusted off the soft snow and straightened out her lovely new red coat. She could feel herself trembling slightly with anticipation.

"Now, all you have to do is look into the eyes of the statue. Keep looking and something will change. It's nothing scary so don't worry."

Bertie did as instructed but felt very silly staring at an expressionless concrete man, especially when nothing happened.

"Try again, it may take a little while. Just think of the statue as a real dude." Her cheeks flushed. She glanced sheepishly at Mr Muse who just winked back and nodded towards the Morpheus. Once again, she stared into the stone eyes of the statue but this time they seemed to stare back at her. Then, she felt something – a connection of some kind although she was unsure what it was. Suddenly a bright circle of white light beamed out from the eyes and shone before them like a large, round cinema screen.

"Oh! I wasn't expecting that!" she cried, stumbling backwards in surprise.

Mr Muse jumped up and down clapping his hands furiously. "Fantastic! Well done, Bert, you're a natural at this!" he screeched. Realising his overreaction he calmed himself and resumed his teaching. "Sorry, most newbies don't manage that quite so quickly. Now, *this* is called a Gateway. The fact that you can create your own Gateway shows you have the potential to become a Dream Dweller."

"Me?"

"Yes, I mean you're too young to be a fully-fledged one right now but you're never too young to start learning. Do you think you'd like to try it?"

"Well, yes I would, I think. I mean I don't have a clue what you do." She was beginning to feel a little out of her depth.

"Of course, no, no, I haven't shown you much yet but you'll soon see, don't worry," he reassured. "Anyway, let's continue. Now, look into the Gateway. Tell me what you see." The light began to project vivid images before them.

"It's like watching TV!" she laughed. "It's so clear. Oh, that's odd...I can see a little boy in a classroom...teaching lots of teachers. Ha! How funny. Oh, now the teachers are throwing paper aeroplanes at each other. What's all this about?"

"This is a dream that one of my dreamers had the other day which I saved for you. She's a teacher you see, and that particular day she had told one of her pupils off for calling her lesson boring. I believe her words to him were, 'If you think you can do better, you have a go.'"

"Ah right, so she had a funny dream about it that night."

"That's right," he confirmed. "It's what Dream Dwellers call an 'Earth Influenced Dream'. They quite often consist of jumbled nonsense but they help our brains sort out the events that have taken place in our lives. It's a bit like filing things in the right place and filtering out the rubbish. Most people don't remember them the next morning because they're not overly important."

Bertie nodded and chuckled in recognition. She'd had plenty of those although she tended to remember all of her jumbled nonsense.

"But," he continued, "Sometimes people have obscure or dramatic dreams because they are in need of help. It could be that they have family issues, perhaps they are being bullied, or they are simply sad or lost in some way. Whatever it is, we need to help them and we do this in two ways. We can intercept a dream that a person is having and change the ending to ensure a positive outcome or we create dreams to ensure they get a specific message or a sign, which will help them. Now these are called 'Morpheus Dreams.' They require great skill and only experienced Dream Dwellers can achieve this."

"I can't believe you become part of people's dreams, that's so awesome," Bertie sighed, hanging onto his every word.

"So, to summarise, when Dream Dwellers see dreams through Morpheus, they can analyse them, they can intercept them and, they can create or shape dreams to help people on earth, just as Morpheus did many, many years ago."

"I see," she said with a look of wonder. "So how do you know when someone needs help?"

"Well, let's look at a dream that your dad had a short while ago and then I can explain."

"My dad? Why my dad?" she exclaimed.

"Well now, this is the reason that you're here, Bertie. I thought perhaps you could start to learn how to be a Dream Dweller by helping me to help your dad. I'm his Dream Dweller you see. I thought it would be a good way for you to learn as it should be easy for you to interpret his dreams."

"But why does my dad need help? I mean I know he's a little bit 'out there' but we love him for his crazy ways. Is he OK?"

Mr Muse chuckled. "It's nothing we can't fix so please don't be alarmed, he's just lost his way a little and he needs some help finding the right path, that's all."

"Lost his way?" she repeated. She couldn't help but worry despite Mr Muse's assurances.

"Please don't fret. He's wonderfully happy at home, he couldn't be happier than when he's with his family. His *work* is where his discontentment lies. His job is leaving him very unfulfilled and dissatisfied and it's beginning to affect him. He's started to lose his spark, have you noticed that?"

"I have," Bertie nodded solemnly. "I noticed it tonight for the first time and I have to say, it worried me. He won't admit he's unhappy though. He says he's lucky to have a job at all, so I guess he doesn't see the point in complaining."

"And that's the problem, he's not seeing the bigger picture." Mr Muse gestured towards the glowing Gateway. "Shall we have a look and see what's going on in his dreams? Perhaps it might illustrate how he's feeling." Bertie nodded but she was apprehensive. What if she saw something that worried her more?

"OK, tell me what you see in the light," he instructed, gazing up at the glowing circle.

Bertie watched as 3D images of her dad came to life in the Gateway. She saw he was in the middle of an open plan office. Everyone around him was working hard at their desks, seemingly oblivious to his existence, but on closer inspection, she saw that her dad was in fact sitting on a toilet - naked - smack bang in the middle of the office. He was desperately trying to hide himself from his colleagues but there was no way of escaping the excruciating embarrassment. Weirdly though, no one in the office seemed to notice him.

"Oh! Oh!" Bertie exclaimed. "My poor dad! Why is he naked? Why is he on the loo in front of all of those people? That's awful!" Then she started laughing and she couldn't stop. She wondered why Mr Muse wasn't laughing. Was he not seeing what she was seeing?

"Ahh, this is a classic dream, I've seen this a million times. What do you think it means?" he asked all too seriously, his arms folded across his chest.

"That my dad is asleep and he needs to go to the toilet?" she smirked.

"No, good try but it's much deeper than that. It actually means that your dad is feeling very exposed right now."

"I'd say!" Bertie giggled. "You can't get more exposed than naked in front of your boss!"

"Exactly," said Mr Muse. "This sort of dream shows that your dad feels his ability to do his job is being questioned. Is he good enough to get the job done? Does he have the skills to be in charge of people? I think perhaps his boss is making him feel he can't cope with the new workload and your father is doubting his own ability." Bertie swapped her smile for a frown. It did all seem to make sense to her. "Let's look at another dream that he had recently which will illustrate this further."

Mr Muse put his hand in the Gateway and swished it to the right. The picture changed and they watched as Mr Brownlee was seen looking straight at them. He stepped forward until his face filled the Gateway. He appeared to be studying his appearance in a mirror and he smiled broadly to check his teeth. Suddenly his happy expression switched to absolute horror. Bertie jumped.

"Oh my goodness, his teeth are falling out!" She watched as tooth after tooth fell from his lips. Her poor dad clasped his hands to his mouth in a vain and desperate attempt to hold his teeth in place but one by one they loosened and dropped to the floor. It was a very sorry sight.

"Just remember this is not real, it's just what's going on in his mind. His teeth are still firmly in his head," smiled Mr Muse. Bertie sighed and smiled too.

"So does this show that he's feeling worried about his job as well?" she asked.

"It's another classic one that we call an insecurity dream." He sensed her confusion. "To be insecure means that you don't feel safe or comfortable, maybe because you're anxious or worried about your position in life."

"I see, yes, you would be terribly worried if your teeth fell out!"

"Being naked or losing your teeth or hair are very common dreams. We all feel a little wobbly in life at times."

They watched as the images faded and the glowing light of the Gateway slowly dissolved. The two of them decided to take a stroll towards the cobbled street and the quaint little shops as the snow danced around them.

"So what happens now then?" Bertie asked, kicking up snow with her little black shoes.

"Well, what needs to happen next is for your dad to admit he's not satisfied with his job and take action to make changes. If he doesn't, his discontentment may turn into deep unhappiness and possibly depression. If this happens, he may find himself out of work which would affect your whole family."

"Right," said Bertie glumly. "I can't bear the idea of Dad becoming depressed, that's so unlike him."

"But it can happen to anyone who becomes stuck and unable to find a way out, even someone as naturally happy as your dad."

Bertie fell silent. She felt slightly sick. The thought of her dad keeping a job that he hated and could potentially make him ill caused her great sadness. Mr Muse sensed this and was quick to reassure her once again.

"Fear not, young Bert, help is at hand. My job is to stop anything untoward from happening. Once he's ready to make a change we'll concentrate on finding out what the right career path is for him and make sure he follows it. But we need to act fast so that we can work on changing the course of events to create that all important happy ending."

"So what can I do to help?"

"You could speak to your dad about his job and try to get him to admit to himself how he's feeling. That would be a real help."

"Consider it done, Mr Muse. I shall report back to you tomorrow with my findings." Her mood lightened with this new purpose.

"Marvellous!" he smiled. "But, he may not know how to make the necessary changes or he may be too scared and that's where things get far more interesting for us."

"Really? Is that when we'd get to intercept his dreams?" A sudden peculiar tingling rippled through Bertie's body, making her rather light-headed. This was followed by the strangest pulling sensation as though her soul was being tugged from her body. "Oh!" she exclaimed, "what's happening?"

"Ah, my child, it's time for you to go now, you are fading. I know it's been a lot to take in but I do hope to see you again tomorrow. We'll be here to greet you when you return. And remember this, it's absolutely vital that Dream World is kept a secret from anyone on earth otherwise our work here would be destroyed." He tapped a long pointy index finger to his closed lips and gave a wink. Bertie acknowledged this with a knowing smile and a thumbs-up. Who'd believe her anyway?

The D-zone with her charming Christmas cottage and the cobbled street and the warm dry snow swiftly drifted further and further away until eventually they were out of sight.

Back, back she tumbled.

Back to earth.

Back to her other life.

CHAPTER 10

"Wake up, Darling," called Mrs Brownlee. "Dad's leaving for work soon, I thought you might want to have breakfast together before he goes."

It took a few moments for Bertie to realise where she was when she awoke the following morning. She prized open her eyes and as they gradually focused, she spied the beautiful red and gold Christmas tree and the pretty little fireplace. She felt the unfamiliar marshmallow pillows and the bouncy duvet that cocooned her body and she smiled as she remembered the opulent luxury of the Barnes house.

It took a few moments more to compute all of the events of her…dream? Oh goodness, was it a dream? Yes, yes it must have been. She was pretty sure it was - a very vivid and intricate dream. One of the most surreal by far and *so* fantastically detailed. She lay in the bouncy marshmallowness, feeling an overwhelming sense of deflation. Her wild adventure had all been just an incredibly elaborate fantasy. Of course Dream World wasn't real. How could it be? She reviewed every aspect of the dream in her mind and her deflation eventually turned to contentment. She'd had an incredible experience, even if it had been imaginary.

Pulling back her curtains, Bertie glowed inside as she gazed out upon an opaque Barnes yet to be touched by daylight. She knew most people moaned about the darkness of the December mornings but to her it made everything all the more festive, especially as her mum had turned on the Christmas lights that linked across the garden fence below. It looked so very pretty, almost as delightful as the Christmas Tudor house in her dream.

She padded down the bouncy carpeted staircase and into the kitchen to join her family at the huge oak table.

"You're very quiet this morning, my little world of gorgeousness." Her dad squeezed her tightly and planted a big kiss on the top of her head before handing her some buttery toast and a big glass of milk. "Did you sleep ok, Hen?"

Bertie stared at her dad. His teeth were still in his head. That was good.

"I had a lovely sleep thanks, Dad. I had the weirdest dream ever though..." She was about to tell her parents the details of the ridiculously surreal dream when her dad abruptly interrupted her flow.

"Oh! You've just reminded me!" he said, dramatically. "I had this horrible dream last night. I was on the toilet in front of everyone in my office. Right in the middle of the office! And not only that, I couldn't get off it because, well, I was naked! Can you imagine?!"

Mrs Brownlee gave a shriek of laughter and Billy found the idea of Daddy on a toilet totally hysterical.

Bertie's mouth fell open.

"Oh it was awful!" Mr Brownlee added. "I was so relieved when I woke up this morning and realised it was just a dream."

"How funny," Mrs Brownlee sniggered.

"I know," he continued. "Plus, the other night, I dreamt that all my teeth fell out *and*, a few nights ago, I dreamt that my hair fell out! What's all that about?"

Her mum and Billy laughed hysterically at the idea of Dad with no teeth or hair. Bertie had dropped her toast. She sat staring at her dad in complete shock.

"You ok, Hen?" he asked, staring back at his daughter. "Is the idea of a bald, gummy, naked, toilet squatting Dad too much for you at this hour of the day?"

Ignoring her Dad's banter, Bertie peeped inside her pyjama pocket and there, as bold as day was the bright pink flower from Stella's garden. Her heart pounded. She sat in stunned wide-eyed silence as the reality of last night dawned on her.

Dream World was real! Very, very real.

"What's the matter, Darling?" her mum asked. "You've gone very pale."

Bertie was stunned into silence. She had to force herself to speak so as not to give the game away.

"Oh…errr…nothing…no, no…it's just that I…I…was trying to remember what you call those types of dreams."

"I think they just mean that you're worried about getting old," Mrs Brownlee joked as she smoothed her husband's bed hair.

"I'll have you know I'm in my prime. A fine specimen of a man and you're a very lucky woman to have someone as handsome and this."

Bertie's head was spinning. It was all too much to take in and she even wondered if she was still dreaming. Then she remembered what Mr Muse had told her last night about helping her dad and she pulled herself together. She had to act fast and strike while she had the chance.

"That's it!" she blurted, raising a knowing finger in the air. "They are called insecurity dreams. It means that you're feeling exposed in some way or worried about your place in life. Sometimes it's a sign of unhappiness - maybe at work, perhaps?" Her voice trailed off and it was her dad's turn to stare opened mouthed at her. She had obviously hit a nerve.

"Oh how very profound of you. How do you know about this then, Bert?" her mum enquired.

"Uh, oh, erm, the Internet. You know me, I'm always having really mad dreams so I sometimes look up their meanings. The dreams Dad had are quite common apparently."

She hated lying to her parents but she couldn't possibly tell them about Mr Muse in Dream World. They would definitely think she had lost her marbles. Plus, she wasn't about to give away the secret.

Bertie studied her dad. He'd gone strangely quiet. She had made him think. This was good.

"I'd better dash," he whispered as he swigged the last of his tea. "I don't want to be late," and before they knew it he was out of the door.

"Maybe he *is* worried about something," frowned Mrs Brownlee. "I'll have a word with him later."

"I hope I haven't upset him, Mum, I didn't mean to."

"No, no, Pet, don't you worry. Your dad is fine. Come on you two, get ready and we'll take Barry out for a walk. It'll give us the chance to explore our new neighbourhood."

Would he be fine Bertie wondered? Had she just unnecessarily opened up a can of worms and upset her dad or would Mr Muse be proud of her for getting the ball rolling on their quest to set his life straight? She didn't have a clue what to make of anything any more. Everything was far from normal.

CHAPTER 11

When the sun finally rose behind a shield of grey clouds, Bertie discovered that Barnes was just as enchanting as she had imagined and the silvery layer of frost presented a pleasing touch of Christmas. The ground was hard and crunchy underfoot and the icy air turned their breath to clouds.

As they walked, Bertie tried to make sense of everything that had happened the night before. It had all been rather overwhelming. Had she really visited an entirely new world that no one knew existed? She looked at the people who passed her by and wondered if any of them were Dream Dwellers. Was anyone she knew a Dream Dweller? Then she thought of the two amazing new houses in beautiful locations that she'd experienced in the last 24 hours, neither of which was her home. How was she was going to feel when she had to return to their real house after Christmas?

The three Brownlees weaved their way around the Willow trees that surrounded a large, well-established pond in the heart of the village while Barry The Dog had the time of his life exploring his new environment. Unfortunately, he took rather too much interest in a Canadian goose and went hurtling off up the path after it. Bertie had the misfortune of being on the other end of the lead at the time and suddenly found herself pulled to the ground in rather spectacular style by the excitable hound.

Her mum came to her rescue closely followed by Billy who helped her to her feet. Luckily the only damage was to her pride. She dusted herself off while they looked around for Barry. He was spotted in the near distance running round in circles looking for the goose that had long since flown off. Just then, they saw a boy grab the lead to stop Barry from getting into further mischief.

"Thank you so much," panted Mrs Brownlee as they all ran over to reclaim their naughty pup. "He's such a nightmare. Not blessed with brains, this dog."

The boy smiled and handed the lead over to Mrs Brownlee.

"He's gorgeous! What's his name?"

"Homeless," quipped Bertie, still reeling from the embarrassment of face-planting the path. The boy chuckled and threw Bertie a friendly smile. She blushed and smiled back. He looked like a member of a boy band with his on trend clothes and floppy fringe. No one in her school was that good-looking, she was quite sure of it.

"I'm TJ and this is my mum," he said in a very confident and mature manner for a boy of his young years. Standing beside him was a strikingly beautiful woman in a wide brimmed hat, camel coloured wool coat and very expensive looking knee high leather boots. She oozed glamour and sophistication; so much so, Bertie made a snap judgment that she would be unapproachable and unfriendly. How wrong she was.

"Pleased to meet you," smiled the lady as she shook everyone warmly by the hand. Was that an American accent? "I'm Polly. Are you ok, Dear?" she asked, placing a caring hand on Bertie's arm. "Your dog is rather frisky!"

"Oh, I'm fine thank you," Bertie replied, blushing a little more.

"I'm Bea and this is Bertie and Billy," Mrs Brownlee interjected, "and this little fella is Barry."

TJ bent down to make a fuss of Barry. "I'd love a dog like this."

"Well, you can borrow this one as I sure won't be walking him again for a while," Bertie deadpanned. "He's such a big bumbling idiot."

TJ chuckled. "I'm happy to take him out for you if you like."

"Bertie is only joking, TJ, she loves him really. Barry's just over excited because this is all new territory to him," Mrs Brownlee explained. "We've only just arrived here you see. We're staying for Christmas."

"Us too!" said Polly, a little surprised. "We're only here for a couple of weeks to visit TJ's dad. He's been working in Barnes for months now and we haven't seen much of him. We didn't want to be apart over Christmas." Bertie and her mum exchanged surprised expressions.

"That's exactly why we're here too! My husband is working in Richmond and the only way to spend Christmas together was to come and join him."

"Well isn't that a coincidence," laughed Polly. "So it looks like we're both strangers in this village. Fancy joining us on our walk, you guys? Then TJ can take Barry off your hands for a little while, Bertie."

The out-of-towners strolled around the green, avoiding the geese, and chatting like old friends. Bertie found TJ surprisingly easy to talk to and, for someone who never usually spoke to boys, she felt strangely at ease in his company.

"So, your dad's working around here too then huh?" he asked as he threw a stick for Barry.

"Yes, he is but it's only for a short while," she replied. "We live miles away. Where do you live?"

"Oh, all over. Wherever my dad is working at the time, we're there. We've got houses in a few different countries." He was surprisingly matter of fact about the whole thing and Bertie was rather impressed by his lack of arrogance.

"How does that work with school then?" she asked. "Do you still have to go?"

"Well sort of. I have a tutor who comes with us. She's very nice, almost part of the family."

Bertie was intrigued. "So where else do you live then? I can detect a hint of an accent but I can't seem to place its origin. America perhaps?"

"Probably," he shrugged as they strolled along. "I was born in the UK and we spend a lot of our time here but I've also spent a great deal of time in America too – Los Angeles mainly. We have a place in Barbados and one in Ireland as well so we're quite often on the move. I

81

don't really know where to call home and I never think I've got an accent!"

"You have *so* many homes!" Bertie said, enviously.

"Too many," he laughed.

She was dying to know what his dad did for a living but felt it a little too nosy to ask seeing as he hadn't offered the information.

"It sounds like fun, all that travelling around. You're quite the Nomad."

"Yeah, I'm so lucky that I get to see so many different countries but, to be honest, I'd much rather be in one place all the time. My mum and I travel so we can see more of my dad but he works such long hours that we don't really get to see much of him anyway."

TJ gazed down at the ground and scraped some frost off the pavement with his boot. He was suspended in thought and Bertie detected a hint of sadness. She wasn't sure what she should say next and wondered if she'd said too much already.

"Anyway," he said brightening up, "if you guys are around over Christmas we should try and meet up again. It's nice having kids my own age around." Bertie couldn't stop a broad grin from spreading across her face.

"Yeah…erm, yeah, that would be great," she beamed. "But you do realise that I come with a nightmare four year old and a runaway dog don't you?" Just on cue, they heard Billy roaring with laughter and they looked up to see that he had put his gloves on

Barry's front paws. The poor dog was trying to walk with what looked like hands. TJ laughed loudly.

"Somehow I don't think that will be a problem."

CHAPTER 12

Mr Brownlee was sat at a computer frantically uploading software when his boss crashed into the room.

"BROWNLEE!"

Mr Brownlee jumped two foot in the air. "Yes Mr Hardwick!" he quivered. "What can I do for you?"

"What can you do for me?!" boomed the boss. "I'll tell you what you can do for me. You can get these systems up and running a damn sight faster than you're doing right now or else you'll lose this company a shed load of money. THAT'S WHAT YOU CAN DO FOR ME!!"

Mr Hardwick had turned an unusual shade of pinkish purple. He stomped over to where Mr Brownlee was sitting, slapped his hands angrily on the table and leant forward until the two men were practically nose to nose.

Mr Brownlee began to perspire.

Mr Hardwick lowered his voice to a harsh whisper.

"You're not on some little holiday you know, Brownlee, you're here to work," he spat, his baggy face snarling with rage. "I don't know what you and your team have been doing all this time but this needs to be finished in a little over a week and you've only just started."

Normally, Brian Brownlee would not allow anyone to speak to him like this. Back in the days when he was single and carefree, he would have told this hideous Hardwick bloke what he could do with his thankless, unrewarding job. But not any more, not now that he had a family to support. Despite hating his job and hating this despicable idiot, he had to keep his cool and it was one of the hardest things he'd ever had to do. He took a deep breath.

"We've been working flat out since we got here, Mr Hardwick." He was aiming to sound confident and in control but he wasn't sure he was pulling it off. "None of us are leaving the office until 9 o'clock at night to try and get it all finished. There's simply so much to do. We're doing our best to..."

Mr Hardwick's baggy, snarling, pinkish purple face now resembled a raging bulldog.

"It's. Not. Good. Enough!" he hissed.

Mr Brownlee blinked hard as sprays of spit hit his eyes. He didn't dare wipe them. He didn't dare move. He didn't trust himself not to stand up and land a punch square on this horrid man's protruding snout.

Mr Hardwick slowly backed off without losing eye contact, like some odd staring competition, and produced an index finger, which he pointed too closely to Mr Brownlee's face.

"If the computers in the offices of this floor aren't set up by the end of tomorrow, you're out of a job!"

With that, he stormed out of the office and slammed the door.

CHAPTER 13

When Mr Brownlee returned home that evening, Bertie and her mum were bursting with excitement about their glamorous new transatlantic friends and couldn't wait to tell him all about their homes in all corners of the world. Mr Brownlee feigned a smile and mumbled something about keeping in with them so that they could bag a freebie holiday to Barbados but his family could tell there was something wrong. His humour was flat and lacked its usual spark and sarcasm.

"You OK, Darling? You look exhausted," soothed Mrs Brownlee as she took his coat.

"Yes I'm fine, it's just been a long day," came his gloomy reply.

Billy studied his dad's face closely for a while. "You don't look like you tonight, Daddy."

"Don't I, Billy? Who do I look like then?"

"I don't know," said Billy, glumly. "You just look…um…all sad."

Mr Brownlee looked down at his cute little blonde haired, blue-eyed boy and his heart melted.

"Well we can't have that now can we?" he said as his frown gave way to a smile. "Come on, let's all hit the Jacuzzi. I need to forget about work."

"But Daddy, it's late," cried Billy. It was hours past his bedtime.

"Well, Buster, it'll be even later if we don't get a wiggle on." Mr Brownlee tickled his son in the ribs making him squeak. "Come on everyone, into your swimsuits, your dad needs to relax. I bet I get mine on first," and with that, Billy and Bertie raced up the stairs, screaming excitedly.

After their late night swim in the rock star spa, as it was now known, Mr Brownlee had returned to his usual sunny self but Bertie wasn't fooled by his behaviour. She could tell he was putting on an act for the sake of his family and this was confirmed when she heard him singing his default song in the bathroom. She called it that because his brain seemed to default to that song any time he was hiding something. He sang it when he'd had a sneaky pint in the pub after work instead of coming straight home and he sang it at full volume when he'd eaten the last of the sweets and blamed his children. Luckily it was a song Bertie liked – one he'd written back in his band days called "Finding My Way Back Home." What was he hiding this time?

She couldn't wait to fall asleep that night and revisit Dream World. She was now on a mission to help her dad find his right path as he was clearly way off it right now.

As soon as her head hit the marshmallow pillow she was out like a light. She knew she was asleep when, once again, she found herself outside her beautiful Tudor D-zone cottage. She was surprised by how comfortable it felt being back; it was like a second home already. As she stood admiring her house for a moment, one of her little reindeer trotted keenly over to welcome her back. She was stroking its velvet fur when a female voice called out to her.

"Ah! Bertie, you're here!"

She had expected to be met by Mr Muse when she returned to Dream World but instead Stella was striding towards her up the cobbled street. She greeted Bertie with a friendly hug.

"Hi, Stella, lovely to see you again." She smelled as sweet as the flowers in her pretty meadow and she reminded Bertie of holidays and summer. Her porcelain skin and dark flowing hair looked so striking against the snowy backdrop. She possessed the warmth of a favourite Aunty, which made Bertie feel protected and safe in this new world.

"I've really enjoyed looking around your D-zone. Have you tried your Morpheus yet?"

Bertie suddenly felt quite grown up at the thought of owning her own Morpheus. She could pretend to be a real Dream Dweller.

"Yes, with Mr Muse yesterday. I saw some of my dad's dreams."

"Ah yes, Mr Muse has filled me in on the events so far. He's going to join us a little later. How has your dad been today?"

"Not good," Bertie sighed. "He reacted strangely this morning when I mentioned that he's been having insecurity dreams, which proves that he's struggling with work and he's pretending to be happy when I can tell he's not."

"Well we don't want him to be off course for long do we? Let's get straight to work and see what we can find out tonight. Maybe we can help him a little."

They sat down in the warm snow and positioned themselves in front of the Morpheus. Once again, Bertie stared into the eyes of the statue until she had created the circular white glow of her Gateway. Stella was most impressed at Bertie's natural ability and told her as much.

Almost instantly more images of Mr Brownlee appeared before them. They both giggled as they watched him talking to a large bull with his boss's face on it. This was swiftly followed by other dreams involving Uncle Andrew in the Jacuzzi and a giant alarm clock on a beach in Barbados.

"These Earth Influenced dreams seem really random but they show how unsettled he's feeling right now," noted Stella. "I could analyse them for you but they're not too important. Keep watching as something is about to happen."

It wasn't long before the atmosphere of his dreams took a dramatic turn. They watched as Mr Brownlee found himself standing on a tiny square piece of wood not much wider than his feet. For a reason they couldn't fathom, he appeared to be petrified - frozen to the spot with his arms stretched out as it to steady himself. It was then that the scene zoomed out to reveal the piece of wood on which Mr Brownlee stood was balancing precariously on top of an incredibly tall and ridiculously thin pole which took him way up into the misty clouds. His right knee twitched and this slightest of movements sent the pole wavering around in the sky like a fragile long-stemmed flower flailing in the wind. By now he was crouching down, gripping the tiny square of wood beneath his feet so desperately his knuckles had turned white and he was making a peculiar dog-like whimpering sound. His whole body had begun to tremble uncontrollably, which made the thin pole swing wildly in every direction. He was going to fall. He knew it. It was only a matter of time. His paralyzed body hung on for dear life to the world's cruellest fun fair ride; a hopeless, solitary figure stranded and helpless.

He tilted his head very slightly towards the ground below and spotted people, like tiny ants, gathering at the bottom of the wavering pole. He tried screaming to them for help but frustratingly, he made no noise. He opened his mouth wider and tried again, almost retching as he forced his throat to make a sound – any sound to alert the people, but still nothing. He knew that without their help he would surely die. One slip and that would be his end.

Then out of the despair, a small voice could be heard from the crowd of people below. A small voice with a very clear message. "You won't fall, you're ok. You just have to be brave. You have the strength to get through this on your own."

Mr Brownlee registered the words of reassurance but could do nothing in response. He took a long, deep breath and exhaled slowly.

"That's it, just breathe. That's all you have to do," came the voice again. "Just take your time, slow and steady and you'll get there. You're doing great. You can do this."

Mr Brownlee took another deep breath followed by another slow exhalation, this time releasing with it the pent up fear and desperation he held in every fibre of his body. Gradually, the pole seemed to stabilise and the tense atmosphere eased.

"That's it, you're doing brilliantly. You can do this," the voice said. "Just breathe away the fear." With each deliberate breath Mr Brownlee took, the pole lowered further and further until eventually reaching the ground. Bertie watched as her dad stepped off and carried on about his business as if nothing had happened. The images dissolved leaving the Gateway empty once again. It was only then that she realised she'd been holding her breath in anticipation and took in a huge gasp of air.

"Gosh, this is like watching a scary movie!"

"He must have woken himself up," Stella frowned. "Let's wait for him to fall back to sleep."

"He probably woke Mum up too," added Bertie, knowing what a light sleeper her mother was. "He'll be back to sleep in no time, don't worry. That man can sleep anywhere. Mum says he could sleep on a washing line if he had to."

Bertie was right. Within minutes, Mr Brownlee was snoring away again and the Gateway flickered back into life. This time the scene was some sort of lush green tropical jungle, although the images weren't too clear at first. Bertie squinted her eyes.

"What's that he's walking along?"

"I think it's a type of rope footbridge and it looks like it's stretching from one high cliff to another. Look, there's a seriously dangerous drop in between."

Below the footbridge was a three hundred metre sheer drop onto rough, stony ground. It was quite clear that nobody would survive a fall from such a great height.

"Oh!" she exclaimed, "that footbridge doesn't look too safe. And are those storm clouds?"

Stella nodded. "Do you see what's happening here? He has to get across that rotten, hazardous bridge to the cliff on the other side where he will be safe."

They watched intently as Bertie's dad battled against the storm's lashing rain and gushing wind as he frantically tried to haul himself across the rotten ropes, his feet slipping at every step. The rope bridge, intent on expelling its unwelcome guest, presented gaping holes too wide to cross and slime too impossible to gain a firm grip but Mr Brownlee refused to be beaten. He soldiered on, grasping at the slippery ropes and leaping heroically between the missing footings. He was panting with exhaustion as the punishing wind fought against his every step and the rain blurred his vision but he was determined to win the battle. Then as he took another courageous step forward, his foot slipped and his leg plunged through the gap in the footings. The rope bridge flipped sideways, spewing Mr Brownlee off the bridge and launching him into the air like a missile.

"NO!" screamed Bertie, clasping her hands to her face. "This is terrible! What's going to happen?!"

"It'll be ok, just keep watching," Stella said without so much as a flinch.

Bertie couldn't understand how Stella could be so calm whilst watching someone plummet to their death. Her dad was now plunging so fast towards the ground she could hardly bear to watch.

Suddenly, from nowhere, came a flash of golden fur flying at high speed down towards him. It swooped underneath and swept Mr Brownlee skywards like a rocket.

"What is *that*?" exclaimed Bertie. "Is it...a lion?!"

Stella chuckled loudly. "I think it is. Only in a dream would you see a flying wild cat!"

The huge shaggy lion slipped through the sky like a glider with Mr Brownlee loving every moment of the thrill ride. They circled above the fallen bridge and the three hundred metre deep valley below, then Mr Brownlee stretched out his arms and the lion dropped from underneath him, leaving the father of two soaring through the sky like an eagle. Bertie laughed aloud as she heard her dad whoop with the thrill of his empowering flying dream. She knew only too well how liberating that felt and she was glad he had experienced it too.

After much soaring, swooping and loop-the-looping, Mr Brownlee finally made a well-executed landing at his destination of the safe cliff top. He stood tall and proud for a moment, soaking up the euphoria before the dream came to an abrupt end and the Gateway returned to an empty glowing white circle once more.

"Phew!" Bertie panted. "What an intense experience."

Stella nodded, "He's quite the adventurous dreamer, your dad."

As the two girls discussed the events of the dream, the Gateway blinked, causing them to look up. To Bertie's utter astonishment, Mr Muse appeared through the Gateway dressed in unusually casual clothes. He stepped out to join them seated on the ground.

"What? How...how did you do that?" she stammered.

Mr Muse gave a throaty cackle. "Hello Bertie, good to see you again."

"I thought I'd leave you to explain where you've been," said Stella as she gave him a welcome hug.

Bertie made room for Mr Muse to sit down in the warm snow. "Don't tell me you were in my dad's dreams!"

"I was, yes," he confirmed, trying to catch his breath after his exploits. "I felt it was time to intervene tonight. His insecurity dreams were getting rather extreme."

"And, you entered his dream to create a satisfying ending?"

"You're getting the hang of this already," he enthused. He gave Stella a knowing look and the two exchanged satisfied smiles.

"If left unattended, these sorts of dreams tend to leave you with an uneasy feeling the next day, especially if you dream that you are falling. Your dad is obviously suffering from a fear of failure and loss of

control in his job so I needed to show hir
no matter how tough life gets. Flying s'
are on top of things and have risen α
problems. Hopefully he'll now have the strength and
confidence to get through the battles that face him."

"And the lion?" Bertie quizzed.

"Ah yes, that was me! A lion is a fighter of life's
challenges. Rather appropriate I thought. Anyway, you
may begin to see a difference in your dad tomorrow
although I can't guarantee it. We can do our best to
show people signs but it's all down to whether or not
they choose to take note of them."

"That's brilliant! And so clever," said Bertie. There
was a pause. Mr Muse knew what was coming next and
answered the question before she had time to ask it.

"Yes, I've intercepted quite a few of your dreams.
Can you think of anywhere I might have helped you?"

Bertie thought for some time. She'd had so many
dreams that it took a while to review them. "There was
that one I had recently where I was trying to get up a
steep hill to find my dad. I had really heavy legs and
could hardly move them."

Mr Muse nodded. "You mean the one where all
those people were zooming past you at speed?"

"That's the one," she said excitedly. "Were you in
that one?"

"I was the person who stopped to tell you that your
dad was at the top of the hill. I know he'd gone by the
time you got to the top but you still understood the
message didn't you."

"I did," she nodded with a smile. "That was the dream that made me search for the house in Barnes wasn't it? How very clever you are, Mr Muse!"

"Oh the powerful influence of the Dream Dweller," he said with a cheeky wink. "There was also that dream - I don't know if you remember, Bertie - but you were being chased and your feet wouldn't touch the ground?"

"Ahh! Yes, that was so frustrating!"

"Well, I saw off the chasers," he said proudly.

Bertie scratched her head and smiled. "Wow. I remember feeling so scared during that dream but so relieved when I woke up. It's really cool that you can do that."

"We don't think of it as cool anymore do we, Stella? It's just what we do every day so it's normal to us but we still find it exciting and rewarding."

"And sometimes dangerous," Stella added.

"Really? Could you get hurt?" Bertie asked, a little worried.

"No, no, not hurt," Stella said with a frown. "Nothing here can hurt you although it can get a little hairy at times, as you've just seen in your dad's dream. No, the real danger comes when you get stuck in a dream. You need to avoid that at all costs. It's not fun." Bertie noted the serious tone of Stella's voice.

"Stuck?"

Mr Muse picked up from there. "If you've intercepted a dream and that person suddenly wakes up, you are left in their dream. Suspended in animation."

"Oh my goodness! So what happens then?"

"You have to wait until they fall asleep again and sometimes that can be quite a long time. It means that your mind is trapped and your body on earth can't wake up until *they* fall asleep and release you from their dream. That's why you have to be an experienced Dream Dweller to intercept dreams on your own. It can take years of practice."

"Wait, so if you get stuck in someone's dream, that means you stay asleep all day and you're stuck in the dream?" Stella and Mr Muse nodded. "Has that happened to you?"

"It happened to me once," said Stella. "I was trying to help someone who was finding it impossible to make a decision about whether to go to University or accept a really good job offer. They were in complete turmoil and feeling the pressure from their family and friends. Everyone had their opinion and this poor person was so confused they didn't know what to decide. Then they had a very intense dream where they were lost in a maze. They were going round it the wrong way, immersing themselves deeper and deeper into the clutches of the maze. If they had found their way out, they would have been able to make the right decision. I could see this so I intercepted their dream and I was leading the way to the exit with them happily following behind me when all of a sudden they were woken by their dog jumping on the bed."

"Oh no!" Bertie shrieked, biting her lip.

"I know! I was left in this stupid maze, waiting for them to fall asleep again but it was early morning by then and they couldn't get back to sleep."

"So what happened?"

"Well, I was suspended in their dream for a whole day. That maze got more than a little boring after a while I can tell you. I missed an entire day at work; I couldn't even phone in sick because I was asleep! I got into so much trouble the next day with my boss that I came very close to being sacked from my job."

"Oh my goodness, that is terrible." The idea of becoming a Dream Dweller was rapidly losing its appeal.

"The only good thing is that there is no sense of time here in Dream World so even though I was stuck for about 15 hours, it really didn't seem that long. But you try explaining to people why you've been in bed for hours on end without revealing the secret of Dream World – it's not easy."

"So when you've intercepted a dream, how do you know when that person is going to wake up? How do you avoid getting stuck?"

Mr Muse got up from the ground and stretched. Saving Mr Brownlee from the perils of rotten rope ladders and cliff faces had left his muscles a little tired and stiff.

"You don't know," he said in between stretches. "It's something you just get a feel for the more you do it. Depending on what dreams your dad has tomorrow we'll have a go at intercepting one together. What do you think?"

"Well, I..." Bertie stammered. "Possibly." What was she to think? She had just heard how risky the whole business was and then she gets invited to give it a try.

Mr Muse sensed her apprehension. "As long as you stick with me and follow my instruction, you'll be perfectly safe. We'll see how you feel about it tomorrow. I just know we're getting closer to steering your dad onto the right track now and I'd really love you to be part of the experience. But there's no pressure," he said, holding his hands up. "Now, I simply must get out of these casual clothes. I do feel horribly under-dressed without my suit."

There was no doubt about it. Bertie was extremely concerned about being stuck in her dad's dream and not waking up. Her family would be so worried and, worse than that, she'd miss the precious Christmas festivities that she'd waited all year for. But, it wasn't every day that you got to be part of an actual dream.

Could she pass on this experience or was it worth the risk?

CHAPTER 14

Bertie and Billy were surprised to find their father gone and their mother obscured by a huge canvas when they came downstairs the following morning.

"Err...what is going on?" Bertie enquired through bleary eyes. "I don't remember you bringing your painting things with you. And what have you done with our dad?"

Mrs Brownlee peeped out from behind the canvas. She was still in her PJs and her hair was badly tied in a loose, scruffy ponytail.

"Hello Lovelies!" she sang, waving a wisp of hair from her face.

"Your dad couldn't sleep so he went into work early and these aren't mine." She gestured towards a row of blank canvases, tubes of paint and various pallets on the floor next to her. "They belong to Mr Muse. He rang and left a message saying he didn't want them and asked if we could put them to good use. They were locked in a cupboard upstairs. I'm in my element!" She danced around, waving her paintbrush above her head. Bertie rolled her eyes. Not this again.

"Was Dad ok? Why couldn't he sleep?" she asked, knowing full well what had disturbed his slumber.

"I've no idea. He kept waking me up by thrashing about in bed. More weird dreams I think. He seemed ok when he left though. Now, would you be a sweetie and make breakfast for you and your brother?" She waved her paintbrush free hand in the general direction of the kitchen.

"Oh and good news, there's going to be a fundraising fair on Christmas Eve which we can go to. Look, I found this leaflet on the doormat this morning. I thought I'd paint a picture to help raise money for the auction."

Mrs Brownlee handed Bertie the leaflet which she read aloud:

BARNES FESTIVE FUNDRAISING FAIR
CHRISTMAS EVE
2pm
Come and join us for an afternoon of festive fun
Auction to raise money for the Hospice
Tea, coffee and homemade cakes followed by
Christmas Carols around the tree.
Stay for our annual family party:
Live music and dancing, **7pm until late**
All Welcome!
(Please bring your cakes and kind donations for the
auction to the hall before 12pm on the day).

Billy was particularly excited and joined his mother in dancing around the conservatory. Bertie suspected it was because he'd misinterpreted the word 'fair' for the type with rollercoaster rides and stalls where you win oversized teddy bears.

She was excited about it too but she'd really wanted to quiz her dad about his dreams last night and didn't think she could wait a whole day to find out if Mr Muse had worked his magic. Now her mother was in one of her crazy painting frenzies and that spelt disaster for her and Billy. She would often become so preoccupied with creating an inspired work of art that all her motherly duties usually left the building. Luckily, Bertie was experienced in the matter and after breakfast she went about making sandwiches for lunch to prevent them all from certain starvation. She also took the liberty of arranging for TJ and Polly to come over to keep them company. Perhaps if Polly were present, her mum would refrain from singing her default song *all* day while she painted. Creativity was her mum's default song trigger and, as much as Bertie adored songs by Adele, she didn't much enjoy them being sung on constant loop by her out of tune parent.

When their guests arrived a few hours later, Polly followed Mrs Brownlee into the conservatory for a painting master class while the youngsters made straight for the games room.

TJ was suitably impressed by the array of musical instruments on offer and, without asking, helped himself to an acoustic guitar. Bertie loved the way he made himself at home; it really put her at ease in his company. He plopped himself down on a swivel stool and ruffled his fringe in such a cool way, it caused Bertie to stare at him a little longer than was socially acceptable. Oblivious, he slung the strap of the guitar over his shoulder and began tuning the strings.

"Do you play?" she asked him, as casually as she could manage.

"I do, but shhh. Don't tell anyone. My dad would kill me if he found out."

"What do you mean?" she asked, setting up the microphones and amps.

"He doesn't approve of me learning an instrument. I think he's worried that I'm going to want to become a rock star when I'm older. He wants me to be a lawyer or a doctor."

"Oh right. And do you? Want to be a rock star I mean." TJ held the guitar so naturally it almost seemed part of him.

"Well it beats being chained to a desk all day I guess. Thing is, Dad says that creative people, like musicians and artists, are always a bit crazy." Bertie thought of her mother's painting frenzies and was inclined to agree. "He says creative people see the world in a much more complex way than the rest of us which causes them to over analyse things. He thinks they are never at peace with themselves and that creativity never brings happiness."

"Wow, that's such a negative view, I wonder why he thinks that? My mum's an artist and, yes, she loses it a bit when she paints but she's also one of the most grounded people I know."

TJ shook his head. "All I know is that he'd go mad if he knew I'd been on the internet teaching myself to play when he's away."

"How do you hide the guitar?"

"Oh, err, well, it's actually his, but I always put it back so he doesn't know I've used it."

"I see," said Bertie indignantly. "So it's alright for him to play it but not for you? That doesn't sound very fair."

TJ gave a loud sigh. "I know, but like I said, he just wants the best for me. Mum's great 'cause she lets me play whenever I want and she doesn't tell him. It's our little secret. As I told you before, I hardly see him so it's not difficult hiding it from him."

"So, is your dad creative? What does he do for a living?" As soon as Bertie had uttered the words, she wished she hadn't. Given their obvious financial wealth it somehow seemed so rude. She bit her lip nervously and awaited a response. TJ fiddled with his hair and avoided eye contact.

"He err…he err…computers…he writes stuff."

"Oh my dad works with computers too! Maybe they do the same job."

"Maybe," said TJ, clearly not wishing to elaborate. "Your dad obviously earns good money if you can afford to stay in a house like this."

"No! No, no he doesn't," she protested, suddenly realising her error. Of course there was no way their dads shared the same career. "No we're just house-sitting over Christmas. Our home is tiny."

Bertie was now left with a nagging doubt that TJ had only liked her because he thought she was as rich as him. Her heart sank a little. There was a small silence before TJ ended it with a strum on the guitar.

"I love small houses," he said. "They're so homely. Our house in L.A. is mahoosive and there are so many rooms that we don't even use. I always feel a little bit lost in it. I mean, it's fantastic and it's nice to have your own pool but I'd much rather live in a cosy little cottage than a big mansion."

Even though she knew he probably wouldn't rather live in her tiny house, she was touched by his mindfulness. She wanted to give him a big hug for not being judgmental and for accepting her for who she was but she really didn't know him well enough to do that.

He continued to strum the guitar randomly. "What music do you like?" he asked.

"All sorts. Anything. But I especially love female singers with big voices. Dad and I listen to music a lot together. Sometimes he plays the guitar and I, well, I sing."

"You're so lucky that you can do that with your dad, I'd give anything to do that with mine." Bertie noticed a hint of pain in his voice and his gaze met the floor. "I shouldn't complain about my life because I know how privileged I am," he said quietly, "but I'd much rather spend time with my dad than spend the money he earns. Time with your family is worth far more than anything money can buy."

Bertie felt a pang of guilt for mentioning the closeness she shares with her dad when TJ had already expressed how little he sees of his. How could she have been so insensitive? Strangely, she found herself feeling like *she* was the privileged one. Something told her that TJ envied her more than she envied him.

"Have you tried telling your dad how you feel?" she suggested. "Maybe if he knew how sad his absence makes you, he'd do something about it. He might think you're happy with the way things are."

TJ shook his head. "Nah, it wouldn't change anything. He's too in demand…" his voice trailed off into deep thought. Another silence followed. This time Bertie filled it.

"Well, you can come and jam with us if you like. Dad would love having another guitarist to drown out my singing." TJ's face cracked a smile and he looked up at her under his floppy fringe.

"Is your singing that terrible?"

"My friends at school seem to think so. They made fun of me when I sang at the nativity."

"I bet it's not that bad. Go on, sing something for me now, Bertie, I'd love to hear you."

"No, I don't much feel like singing these days." The cutting comments from her classmates pierced her mind like a poisoned dart. She couldn't risk being laughed at again. She quickly turned the focus back on TJ. "Anyway, please, play me something. You know you want to."

"Ok," he said, "but I need one of these." He carefully placed the acoustic back on its stand and reached for the much-coveted Stratocaster electric guitar. He slung the strap over his shoulder and plugged the lead into the amp. As he took a moment to check the tuning and get a feel for the sound, Bertie observed how professionally he handled the guitar – as though he'd handcrafted it himself. This boy knew what he was doing.

Without warning TJ launched into a medley of the most famous guitar riffs in history, ranging from The Rolling Stones to Nirvana to Blur. His fingers effortlessly glided over the frets and strings, plucking and strumming with the skill and expertise of someone three times his age and experience. He was flawless. He was awesome. He completely blew Bertie away. This boy was a genius guitar hero.

"Oh My Word!! You rock!!" she gushed. It was TJ's turn to blush and he ruffled his floppy fringe again, this time to hide his face. "You have to let your dad hear you play, he'd be so immensely proud of you!"

"No I couldn't risk it, Bertie, he'd go mad if he thought I'd gone behind his back."

"But this incredible talent cannot go undiscovered. Right!" she said in her most commanding voice. You and I have *got* to do something about this. I don't know what, but we have *got* to do something."

TJ laughed. "I love a girl with a firm plan."

Bertie thought for a moment then drifted off into one of her daydreams. She hadn't had many since arriving at the Dream House and TJ found it a little unnerving.

"Bertie? Bertie?" he said, snapping his fingers close to her face to wake her up.

"I've got it!" she shouted, making him jump.

"I have got the most fantastic plan ever! *We* are going to write a song especially for your dad and you

107

are going to perform it at that Christmas Fair on Christmas Eve. Genius idea or what?!" TJ went quiet for a moment then shook his head, mournfully.

"No, no, the minute he heard me playing guitar in front of people he'd hit the roof. There'd probably be an ugly scene and no one needs that at Christmas."

"But don't you see? He'll be so mesmerized by your talent. Plus he'll be so touched that you wrote a song for him, there's no way he'd be cross."

Another broad smile crept across TJ's lips as he came round to Bertie's idea.

"Actually, my fabulous friend, you may possibly have come up with a genius plan." But then his face fell and his shoulders slumped. "There's only one problem though. How on earth do we get a workaholic, antisocial, reclusive man like my dad to go to a village festive fair?"

CHAPTER 15

"BROWNLEE!! WHERE DO YOU THINK YOU'RE GOING?"

Everyone working in the offices froze. Silently, they put down their tools and stared at Brian Brownlee in sheer disbelief. He was heading out of the door. Early!

He stopped and turned around to face his boss striding towards him huffing and puffing like a raging grisly bear. Mr Hardwick was furious and he was about to blow.

Mr Brownlee took a big deep breath. "Mr Hardwick," he said with as much authority as he could muster. "I got here at 6 o'clock this morning. It is now 7 o'clock in the evening, which means that I have worked flat out for 13 hours without a break. We have installed all of the computers on this floor today, just as you requested, and are now well ahead of schedule. Therefore *I* am going home to my family."

His colleagues drew a collective sharp intake of breath. No one had dared stand up to this monster of a man for fear of humiliation or instant dismissal despite his repeated bullying of the staff. But, for some reason, Brian Brownlee had discovered a hidden inner strength today and he was ready to challenge the beast. The two men stood nose to nose; one considerably larger than the other. It was like David and Goliath (Mr Brownlee being David - definitely not Goliath).

"NO ONE LEAVES THIS OFFICE BEFORE 9PM!!" The booming anger of Mr Hardwick's voice reverberated around every corner of the office. A thick, heavy tension hung in the air like a thundercloud ready to unleash the mother of all storms. Then, just to add to the tension, he dropped his voice to his trademark vicious, spitty whisper.

"I don't care what time you crawled in here this morning, you cretinous little vermin, you are not leaving until I say so."

The silence was deafening. Nobody dared move. Mr Brownlee took another deep breath and exhaled slowly. He stared Mr Hardwick straight between the eyes.

"13 hours without a break. I'd say it's against the law to make employees work under those kind of conditions, especially without the correct overtime payment. Now I'm sure if I contacted the union they would be very interested in the way you are running things here. In fact, I'm quite sure they would be very keen to pay you a visit and may even make you pay damages to each and every one of your employees here. Things could get very messy, and you don't want that now do you, MR HARDWICK. Now, if you'll excuse me, I've got a family to spend time with."

And with that, he left.

CHAPTER 16

Darkness had fallen early that evening and, much to Bertie's delight, Barnes village had been sprinkled with a fine, silvery mist. She ran around flicking on the Christmas lights in every room. Then she turned off the house lights and, with the help of her mum, lit some candles to create the perfect festive atmosphere. Oh how she loved putting on a DVD and being snug and cosy inside with the roaring open fire and the twinkly lights for company while Jack Frost worked his magic outside. This was the best feeling in the world. This was the feeling she longed for all year round. In the middle of summer when everyone else was having fun playing on the beach or eating picnics in the sunshine, Bertie dreamed of moments just like this. *This* was when she was at her absolute happiest, the moment when everything was right with the world. She savoured every second.

After dinner in front of the TV, her mum brought in a pile of Christmas nibbles and hot chocolate. Bertie thought she might actually burst with bliss. The only thing that would make it ridiculously perfect was if it started snowing and her dad arrived home early.

Just at that moment, the living room door burst open and Mr Brownlee made a game show host entrance.

"Hi everyone! I'm home!" he cheered, throwing his arms open wide.

111

Not expecting this premature arrival, his family leapt to their feet to greet him.

"That is too spooky," Bertie muttered under her breath. "I don't suppose it's snowing outside is it?"

Mr Brownlee embraced his loved ones in a group hug.

"You're home so early, Daddy and you look like *you* again," yelled Billy, excitedly.

"I *am* me again, Billy," said Dad, picking up his son and holding him high in the air until his head scraped the Christmas garlands.

"Why are you in such a good mood, Darling?" asked his wife with a hint of suspicion. "Has something happened?"

Mr Brownlee puffed out his chest with pride. "Well, put it this way, I put nasty Mr Hardwick in his place today and I feel epic! It's no more Nice-Guy-Brownlee. That boss isn't going to push me around any longer."

"You didn't punch him did you, Dad?" Bertie asked, tentatively.

"No, I didn't punch him," he laughed, "although, I've wanted to many times over the years. No, I'd just had enough of his bullying ways and for some reason today I snapped."

Bertie fought hard to hide her excitement. She knew exactly why her father had snapped and it was all down to Mr Muse's hard work last night.

"Oh, Darling, what happened?" asked his wife with concern. "Sit down, sit down! Tell us all about it." She took off his coat and ushered him into the room. The family plumped themselves down on the squishy sofas and snuggled up together drinking their hot chocolate while Dad recounted his stand off with his evil boss. Bertie hid a huge grin behind a fluffy sofa cushion. She so wished she could tell her dad why he felt strong enough to confront Mr Hardwick and had to bite her lip to refrain from revealing her night time secret.

"Why would he get so mad at you for leaving on time?" asked Mum. "You've done so many extra hours at this new place."

"Bea, that man is a monster," he answered. "I've seen before how he's ruined people's lives by sacking them and leaving them penniless. He thrives on other people's misfortune and he enjoys making grown men cry. He gets away with it because we are all too scared of losing our jobs. I've been stressed out for some time now worrying about it but I haven't wanted to burden you all with my unhappiness. I didn't want you to worry."

Mrs Brownlee gave her husband another hug. "Darling, I had no idea you were so unhappy. I didn't realise just how nasty this Hardwick man is. I feel like giving him a piece of my mind and I can't believe you haven't let rip at him before!"

"Believe me it's been the hardest thing in the world not to lump that man one over the years," smiled Dad, "but I didn't because we need the money. I'm sure he'll be furious with me tomorrow but I don't care. I just feel like…like everything will be OK."

'Bingo!' thought Bertie. This was a Dream World triumph. She couldn't wait to tell Mr Muse how much progress her dad had made. He would be overjoyed.

"I think I've finally seen the light. It's time I manned up and got out there and looked for another job – possibly another career. No more bullying bosses. No more computers!"

"Well, we'll find a way of getting through this," said Mum warmly, grabbing his hand and squeezing it tightly. "Billy will be starting school soon so I can go back to work. We'll do whatever it takes to keep our heads above water. We'll be fine, OK? So you mustn't worry."

Mr Brownlee lifted his arm and placed it lovingly around his wife's shoulder. "That's why I married you," he whispered.

"Yuck!" cried Bertie. "Please don't start kissing! That's disgusting!" Her parents laughed and kissed all the more. "So, what do you think you'll do now then, Dad?" she asked, desperately trying to put an end to their display of affection.

"No idea!" he laughed, shrugging his shoulders.

"Well Darling, like I said, whatever you decide to do, we'll support you," said Mum. "Just so long as you don't try and become a rock star again."

"Were you a rock star, Daddy?" asked Billy excitedly. Mum sniggered.

"No, no!" chuckled Dad, awkwardly. "Well, I was in a band when I was younger and I thought we were going to be rock legends but unfortunately things didn't turn out that way." He glazed over for a moment and

Bertie knew that he was reliving the years of hidden hurt from his failed attempt at pop stardom. A year or so ago he'd told her about how he was once the front man of a band called Stryder. He'd been so animated when he'd described how it felt to be the singer, thrashing out his own songs on an electric guitar and rocking a crowd of cheering fans. He'd modelled himself on his idol, Tiger Jonz from the Wildcats. Bertie had been brought up on Tiger's music and many times had witnessed the embarrassment of her dad trying to emulate his idol's high leg kicks and split leaps. He could never quite pull that off. Apparently, her dad's band had been signed to a major record label but just when they thought their path to rock stardom had been paved with gold the label was bought out by a bigger company who proceeded to drop Stryder like a hot potato. His dreams were shattered and his life's worth of songs went unrecorded. Her mum later told her how humiliated he'd felt and how he couldn't face his family and friends for some time. Everyone had had such high hopes for him.

"It's so sad that your dreams were crushed, Dad." As soon as the words had left her mouth, she regretted it. "Sorry, I didn't mean to bring it all back."

"Uh! No worries, Bert, I'm so over the whole pop star thing now. In the long run, the band falling apart was the best thing that could have happened to me. I'd not long met your mother and it gave us the chance to spend a lot of time together. She'd just left art college so we took the summer off and went travelling for a bit, which was an incredible experience. Then soon afterwards we settled down and got married." Bertie glanced over at her mum who was gazing lovingly at her husband.

"I've been so amazingly happy ever since and having you and Billy has put everything into perspective. If I'd have been famous, I might have made lots of money and maybe even owned a house like this but I may never have found the happiness that I have in my life now. And do you know, I look at some of the successful rock stars that were around back then and now they are either really troubled, penniless or dead." Bertie let out an uncomfortable laugh. She was beginning to feel quite glad he hadn't made it as a pop star too.

"Just because you're famous it doesn't mean that you've got it all, and a happy family life is worth far more to me than everyone knowing who I am. I've got everything I need right here." He gestured towards his loved ones and just on cue, Barry The Dog released a huge doggy sneeze, which sent a stringy spray of dog slobber all over his shoes. Billy and Bertie were in stitches.

"There was you being all heartfelt and serious and your dog snots on your feet, Darling," smiled Mum. "Are you sure we were worth giving up your dream for?"

"I'm not sure now," laughed Dad.

Bertie's thoughts quickly turned to TJ and their conversation earlier that day.

"Dad, do you think creative people can ever be truly happy or do you think they see the world too differently to everyone else?"

Mr Brownlee raised his eyebrows. "Err, I don't know, that could be a reason why some creative people struggle with success I suppose." He reached for a tissue to wipe away the Barry snot. "Why ask? Do you think that too?"

Bertie shrugged. "Not really, it was just something TJ's dad said to him. He doesn't want TJ to learn to play an instrument because he doesn't want to encourage him to be creative. He thinks creative people are always a bit crazy and never find true happiness."

"And TJ is this boy that you've got to know? The rich kid?"

"That's the one," she nodded. "He came over today and we jammed together in the games room. You should hear him Dad, he's a ridiculously talented guitarist, totally awesome. You'd be so impressed. He's taught himself to play but he's had to keep it a secret from his dad because he'd go mad if he found out."

"Maybe his dad just doesn't want his son to become a struggling musician who never makes anything of himself. As I found out all those years ago, very few people make it big. His dad is probably just being protective."

"I know what you mean," Bertie sighed, "but TJ is phenomenally good. I feel quite sorry for him. He hardly ever sees his dad because he's always working but if he could just hear his son play I have a feeling he'd think differently."

"Poor little rich kid. You see, that emphasises my point from earlier. I may not earn shed loads of money but you and Billy are happy and here is a boy who has everything except the one thing he craves."

"I know," she said quietly. "It's a shame; he's such a great person."

"Well if it means so much to you, why don't we invite all three of them round for dinner one evening?" Dad suggested. "I mean, his father sounds like a complete bore but I'm willing to put up with him if it means we can have a man-to-man chat about the positives of guitar playing. What does he do for a living anyway?"

"He's something to do with computers apparently," she answered.

"Is he? Oh that's good," chuckled Mrs Brownlee, sarcastically. "You can both talk shop all evening!"

"Fantastic," sighed Dad, forcing a smile.

"Dad, that smile is about as fake as Donald Trump's tan," Bertie laughed.

"It's fine, Darling. Ask them anyway, he'll probably say no…hopefully."

The Brownlees settled down and watched another DVD with their festive nibbles and refills of hot chocolate. Mr Brownlee was so relieved to have finally shared his feelings about work with his family. It was like a huge heavy weight had been lifted from his shoulders and his anxieties and worries had now eased. Even the thought of dealing with TJ's computer bore dad didn't trouble him.

Bertie's mind, however, was whirring.

"I've had an idea," she said, pausing the film. "Maybe we can invite the three of them to join us at the Christmas Fair and the party afterwards. If we all go together, you could get to know them in a relaxed environment."

"Great idea," said Mum, "I'll speak to Polly to arrange it tomorrow. I've been teaching her how to paint and we're both donating our art for the Christmas charity auction. It'd be good to go together so we can see how much money the paintings raise. I'm sure her husband won't be working on Christmas Eve."

Result! Bertie's plan to help TJ's relationship with his dad was really taking shape. All she and TJ had to do was write a cracking song by Christmas Eve and everything would work out fine.

Now there was just a little matter of helping her dad find a new career path. She had a feeling she'd be rather busy in her sleep that night.

CHAPTER 17

Mr Muse was peering in the window of the little toyshop next to Bertie's Tudor house when she arrived back in Dream World that night. She shuffled through the powdery snow to join him and received a shrill greeting and a kiss on both cheeks.

"Bertie, my dear! How are you this fine evening? I was just acquainting myself with your D-zone. It's quite divine."

"Isn't it just," agreed Bertie, gazing at all of the old fashioned wooden toys on display. "I'm very well thank you and I've got such fantastic news too. Shall we go inside and toast some marshmallows by the open fire and I'll tell you all about it."

She so loved her little Tudor Christmas cottage. She had based her whole D-zone on the images she had seen on traditional Christmas cards over the years. She had always envied the little children who peeped in the windows of quaint little toyshops or who held lanterns whilst singing Christmas carols in the old cobbled streets. Now here she was, re-creating one of those famous scenes by toasting marshmallows on the crackling fire with a resplendent Christmas tree beside her and stripy stockings hanging from the mantelpiece.

She told Mr Muse all about her dad's day at the office and his revelation about his desire to leave his job and pursue a new career. He was suitably delighted.

"Oh my! This is such fantastic news!" he gushed. "I didn't expect such an immediate response, I really thought I'd have to fight off dragons or undergo more life saving challenges before he realised his need for change. I have to say, this makes me very happy indeed."

"Well it just shows you how good you are at your job, Mr Muse. It's all very impressive."

Mr Muse became slightly flustered and a little embarrassed by her compliment so he rapidly changed the subject. "Tell me, Bertie, how have you found the portal…I mean, dream house…you know, the one in Barnes? Are you and your family enjoying it?"

"Oh yes it's wonderful!" she enthused. "None of us can quite believe our luck; it's so luxurious. Mum loved the canvases by the way, that was very kind of you to let her have them. She's painting a picture to give to a charity auction on Christmas Eve. It's raising money for the local hospice."

"Well," said Mr Muse, as he speared a marshmallow and warmed it over the leaping flames. "Your mother is a fantastic artist and I knew she'd make good use of them. Have you seen what she's chosen to paint? I think you'll be quite surprised."

"No not yet," Bertie replied as she too spiked another unsuspecting marshmallow. "Mum never likes anyone to see her work until she's happy with it…" her voice trailed off and she was suspended in thought. "Hang on! How do *you* know what she's painting? Have you been back into the house? I mean, I don't mind, it is your house after all."

Mr Muse cackled with laughter. "No, dear girl, I haven't been back to the house I just *know* these things. I know a lot of things."

Bertie watched as he blew on a perfectly toasted marshmallow before popping in his mouth in one go. She was waiting for him to explain *how* he knew a lot of things but no further explanation seemed to be forthcoming, just a lot of chewing. She braved it and pursued her line of questioning.

"So, do you just know these things from our dreams? Or is it, well, is it some sort of...you know...magic?"

He chuckled again, this time a little louder, which caused Bertie some embarrassment. Had she said something really stupid?

"I wish I was a magician! That would be marvellous! Marvellous!!" he shrilled in between chews.

"So how then?" she asked again. She wanted a proper answer.

He drew a deep intake of breath and cast his eyes skywards to contemplate his response. "It's not easy to explain," he said slowly. "There is a force, an energy that exists between earth and Dream World. This energy connects each and every one of us. Most of us go about our daily lives completely oblivious to this energy and others devote their lives connecting to it so they can achieve great knowledge. I guess you could say that I am more in tune with this energy than most, which is why I can see things that others can't."

"Like?" she asked, a little confused.

"Like things from the past, things from the future. I think it's best to leave it at that. I'm afraid I may overload you with too much superfluous information and, at this stage we really should be concentrating on the matter in hand. One day, Bertie, I would love to educate you further as there is so much to explain and I just know you would understand it. Many wouldn't. Now," he said clapping his hands together. "Let's go and see what your dad has in store for us shall we? I have a feeling tonight is going to be a bumpy ride."

Having crammed the last of the toasted gooey sweets into their mouths, they made their way to the Morpheus in the garden. Standing together before the statue in the warm snow, Mr Muse watched as Bertie stared at the winged man until it shone its beam of bright, white light from its eyes.

The circular glow shone motionless for some time. Nothing happened. Mr Muse took this opportunity to encourage Bertie to join him on tonight's adventures.

"So, I'm going to intercept your dad's dreams again and I have a feeling I'm going to have a particularly busy time of it. How do you feel about joining me, are you ready? I could really do with your help."

Bertie chewed the nail on her thumb. She really wanted to join him but was terribly anxious.

"If I get scared, can I leave the dream at any time?" she asked.

"Of course you can. If it gets too much just say and I'll send you back. It's very simple, nothing to worry about. Now remember, you can't get hurt in a dream and nothing bad can happen to you. What happens in the dream appears very real when you experience it from the inside and it can get a bit hairy and scary at times but you must remember, once the dream ends, everything disappears. The only things that remain are the emotions, the feelings and hopefully, the message. OK?"

"I…I…I just don't want to get stuck there, that's all," Bertie stammered.

"I won't let you. You seem to forget Bertie that I am a particularly experienced Dream Dweller!" he said with mock arrogance. "Plus, it's such a thrill! You won't experience anything else like it. It's imperative that you stay close to me though and do *exactly* as I ask. That way you'll be fine. You need to keep your wits about you too as things change pretty rapidly."

Just then the Gateway flickered causing the two of them to look up. Random images danced before them in the glowing circle. Bertie sniggered at the sight of a tabby cat eating spaghetti. She wondered what on earth had triggered that dream. She glanced over at her companion who simply shrugged. She concluded from his silence that even after years of Dream Dwelling, some Earth Influenced dreams defied explanation.

She looked on in awe as the tabby cat began to grow and grow before eventually transforming into an impressively large Tiger. Its orange and black fur shone like silk over its thick rippling muscles. All traces of spaghetti had disappeared and instead, a guitar could be seen placed at the tiger's feet. It lifted its huge, heavy front paw and repeatedly dragged it clumsily across the strings of the instrument. In doing so, the tiger created the most beautiful music. There were no words at first and no real structure to the tune, just enchanting and uplifting music so effortlessly created.

"I think I know what this is about," whispered Bertie, not wishing to disturb the dream. Mr Muse shot her a confused look.

"Really? Do explain as I'm struggling a little with this one. I can't see how it's relevant to your dad's current predicament."

Bertie continued to watch as the Tiger inadvertently created this musical masterpiece. "Dad was reminiscing about his brush with the music business."

"Right," said Mr Muse, none the wiser.

"Well when he was in a band, he wanted to be like a famous singer called Tiger Jonz. He's from a band called Wildcats."

"Ah! I know who you mean, I get the connection now," said Mr Muse enthusiastically.

"Dad has always said what an incredible artist Tiger Jonz is. He reckons he's the best songwriter that's ever lived and that his music speaks straight to your heart."

"Do you like his music too, Bertie?"

"I love it! I just wish he'd write another album soon, it's been ages since the last one and Dad and I are getting a little impatient."

The enchanting music began to pick-up tempo and changed to a cheerful, bouncy tune that Bertie recognized.

"That's Dad's default song!" she squealed. "This is a song he wrote years ago, he sings it all the time. How funny."

Mr Muse smiled to himself and stroked his chin in deep contemplation. He watched for some time as the tiger played the guitar and Bertie sang along. Then suddenly he snapped out of his thoughts, straightened out his waistcoat and corrected his tie.

"Right then, Bertie, I'm going in," he announced. "This is your chance. Are you coming with me?" He held his hand out flat and stared expectantly at her, one eyebrow raised. She felt her stomach fizz and flip. If she didn't go for it now, she was sure she never would.

"Ok, let's do this!" she shrieked and before she had time to change her mind, she grabbed his hand and leapt through the glowing circle of the Gateway with her trusty escort.

CHAPTER 18

Once through the Gateway, a startling flash of blinding white light caused Bertie to recoil. She clasped her eyes shut and shielded them with her free hand, the other holding on a little too tightly to her travelling companion. The next thing she knew, the two of them were sucked forward like metal to a magnet and sent shooting upwards with such velocity, she could feel the skin on her face stretching with the force. After a few seconds everything seemed to slow down and, without any warning, she landed with a heavy thump on solid ground, accompanied by an involuntary scream.

"Oops! I forgot to warn you about that," said Mr Muse apologetically. "That was the transition into the dream dimension, nothing to worry about. Happens every time you go through the Gateway."

Bertie threw him a look of disdain. "Is there anything else you should have told me before I agreed to do this?"

"Probably," he mumbled.

"Great!"

"Right," he said, ignoring her sarcasm, "we're in your dad's dream which is controlled by his mind but some of it will be directed by me so, if I give you instructions, just go with the flow. Do as I ask and whatever you do, don't panic."

"Don't panic? You're worrying me slightly here!" She was debating whether to ask to return to her D-zone right there and then and forget this whole dream interception thing altogether. This wasn't a confident start.

"Just remember, it's only a dream," he reassured, shifting his gaze behind her. "It seems real but it's not. You can't get hurt." He lifted a finger and pointed past her shoulder. "Not even by that creature over there."

Bertie braced herself. Tentatively, she turned around expecting to see the tiger from the dream they'd just watched. Instead her eyes met with a gigantic snarling, snorting grisly bear. It was the size of a large family car and it was heading their way.

Her heart raced and her breath quickened as she stumbled nervously away from the giant animal, it's heavy feet pounding the floor as it lumbered clumsily forwards. Her eyes darted about as she quickly observed her surroundings. They were in some kind of office with her dad and his work colleagues, all of whom were rooted to the spot and shaking in terror at the sight of the beast before them.

"Don't panic," Mr Muse whispered loudly in her ear as he stayed faithfully by her side. "You've nothing to fear. Just stand back out of view and watch."

Bertie took a deep breath in order to regain her composure and the two of them side stepped away from the beast to seek refuge behind a partition. As she peered out from her safe hiding place she repeated the words of her companion over and over in her mind, 'don't panic, it's only a dream.'

Just at that moment chaos broke out. Without warning the bear reared up onto his hind legs and stretched its huge hulking frame skywards. It let out a terrifyingly deafening roar that rocked the building and shattered windows, sending shards of glass shooting across the room like deathly daggers. Bertie yelped with fright and ducked down, covering her head to avoid the flying debris, but escaped unscathed. She glanced up at Mr Muse who stood motionless; his only reaction was an inquisitive frown. All around them, the men in the office screamed like little children as they scrambled under desks and hid behind filing cabinets in an attempt to escape the monster in their workplace. All that is except Mr Brownlee.

Bertie watched in awe as her dad stepped boldly over the broken glass towards the enraged bear. He stood before it with his hands on his hips. The bear took one look at Mr Brownlee and sank its bottom down onto the ground with a thunderous thud that shook the foundations of the building. Then, slowly, it lowered its huge scraggy brown head and sniffed Mr Brownlee's face with its slimy black nose. Its huge lips curled round a clenched jaw as it snarled a dark, rumbling snarl which grew louder and increasingly threatening with every rasping breath it took. Deep, wrathful, fiery eyes stared menacingly into his. Mr Brownlee stood stock still with the bravery of a knight, only turning his head slightly to the side to avoid inhaling the rancid breath of the beast.

Then something extraordinary happened. Mr Brownlee started to sing. He sang softly and quietly, like a father singing a lullaby to his newborn baby. His

129

soothing, calming tones wafted through the air like wispy feathers dancing on a gentle breeze. The great bear ceased its snarling and listened inquisitively to this beautiful sound. So mesmerized by the enchanting voice, it laid its hulking, sweaty body on the floor and swayed its head from side to side. As Mr Brownlee continued to sing, the bear's eyelids slowly grew heavier and heavier and its enormous head drooped lower and lower until finally its nose rested on the ground. Mr Brownlee raised his hand and gently stroked the soft silky fur behind the bear's ears as his melodic voice continued to drift dreamily around the room. Very soon, the bear was slumped in a great heap, snoring loudly.

A collective sigh of relief could be heard from behind various items of office furniture as the colleagues gingerly peeped out from their safe places. Mr Brownlee turned to face his friends as they stumbled over the upturned furniture to hug and thank him. They owed their lives to this great man who had tamed the beast.

Bertie looked at Mr Muse. He said nothing, which was rare for a man of so many words. She knew he was waiting for her to say something first.

"So the bear was Dad's boss, right?" Mr Muse nodded. "And you put the beast there?" He nodded again. "Why?"

"Why do you think?"

Bertie pondered for a moment. "To show him that he is not scared any more?" she suggested.

"Correct. Well done," he smiled. "This man, who your dad once thought of as horrid and fearsome is no longer a threat or a danger to him. He has overcome him. Great isn't it?"

Bertie nodded enthusiastically. "Fantastic! Slightly alarming but exciting too."

"You see, I told you there's nothing to worry about."

Just then the ground beneath their feet rumbled. Bertie looked down and watched as it transformed from a cold office floor to a smooth wide road with bright double yellow lines painted along the side and white intermittent streaks down the middle.

"Oh, we're on the move," said Mr Muse looking around to find his bearings. "You really have to be alert at all times, Bertie, dreams don't hang around."

Bertie scanned the area. "This is our road at home!" she exclaimed. "Look, that's our little house. Oh, and Dad's outside. What's he doing this time?" The two of them watched as Mr Brownlee busily polished the family car on the driveway. Bertie tutted. "He's always cleaning that car. It drives Mum mad."

"I think I would too if my car was white," said Mr Muse. "It's very smart, and new too by the look of it. I suspect it's his pride and joy."

"Hmmm, Mum calls it his third child. He's never had a new car before so he's incredibly precious about it."

"I bet you can't leave crumbs on the back seats," joked Mr Muse.

"Don't be daft, we're not even allowed to eat food in it," smiled Bertie, nudging his arm. She looked back over to her dad and her face suddenly fell.

"Where's it gone?!"

131

"Where's what gone?" Mr Muse swung round to take another look.

"The car! It's gone! Poor Dad, he's looking everywhere for it."

Mr Muse spied the empty driveway and they both spotted Mr Brownlee running up and down the street frantically searching for his precious new white car. Realising what was happening Bertie stopped fretting and turned to her friend.

"Ahhh, I get it. This is one of your interventions isn't it? I think you're going to have to explain this one as I'm not sure I understand it as well as the first."

"Some of what we are about to experience is created by me and some will be your dad's reaction to that. You're just going to have to watch to see how it pans out. Should be interesting," he said with a mischievous grin.

Mr Brownlee took off up the road in search of his car with Bertie and Mr Muse following a safe distance behind, just out of his vision. They pursued him around the neighbourhood before turning off up a narrow, winding country track.

"I've no idea where we are now, this doesn't look like our village any more," Bertie puffed.

"No, we're off on a different tangent. Look, ahead. See those grey clouds? It's all going to get a tad dark from here on in I think."

Bertie shot him a worried look and he gave her shoulder a gentle squeeze. "Remember what I said."

"I know, I know. It's only a dream, nothing can hurt us."

At the end of the winding track was a vast field, which stretched on for several miles. All around was dark and grey now and a heavy feeling weighed down upon them, forcing Bertie to stoop as she trudged on.

"Do you feel that?" Mr Muse whispered as they hung back a little further from her dad. "That intense atmosphere is an exaggerated version of what your dad has been experiencing lately. It will probably get worse as we go on but it won't last. You'll no doubt experience a range of feelings and emotions during the course of this dream."

Bertie was familiar with the power of feelings. She'd often awoken from a dream with little or no recollection of its content but she'd felt sad, worried or anxious for most of the following day as a result.

Over the field they tramped, through long grass and boggy earth. After covering a great deal of ground, Mr Brownlee came to a stop by a lake. He sized it up for a moment before making the bizarre decision not to go around it. Instead, he waded straight in with great intent and determination. Further and further he waded as the water rose higher and higher around him. Bertie and Mr Muse watched from the water's edge as Mr Brownlee came to an abrupt halt in the middle of the lake, the water now up to his waist. Suddenly, they heard him yelling for assistance.

"What *is* he doing?" Bertie stared in disbelief. "What an idiot! Why couldn't he just go *around* the lake? It's not that wide. And why isn't he swimming? He can swim really well." She was exasperated by her dad's actions.

"That lake is thick with mud underneath the water's surface. I'm afraid it's pulling him down. He's sinking." Mr Muse was transfixed by the scene ahead of them. "This is his anxiety about his future. Did you see the way he waded into the deep water with great confidence? That's how he was feeling last night, full of confidence about his decision to leave his dead end job and move on. But this - this is the side of his brain that's questioning that move. This is the doubt, the worry the fear, the 'what if it's all a big mistake?' and the 'what if I can't find another job?' That's why he's stuck in the muddy water. If we don't help him, the doubt and worry will take control and he'll sink further and further down."

"But it's only a dream, he can't die or anything right?" asked Bertie, unable to disguise the quiver in her voice.

"No he can't die but if we don't get him out he'll be left with this intense, dark feeling of doom and he'll wake up tomorrow thinking he's made a big mistake. He'll feel like a failure and he'll have lost the courage he needs to make the positive changes in his life. I'm afraid it's likely he'll stay in that awful job for years and grow increasingly sadder and withdrawn. All of our work up to this point will be undone."

Mr Muse hadn't taken his eyes off Mr Brownlee the entire time and judging by his stern expression, Bertie sensed this was serious.

"We have to help him," he said urgently. "*You* must help him."

"Me? I have to help him?"

"This is why I needed you here in Dream World, Bertie. I can't do this without you."

Bertie felt a sudden injection of pride and importance. "OK," she said confidently, "What do I have to do?"

Just then, terrifying screams for help rang out from the middle of the lake. She turned to see her dad struggling and splashing frantically in the water. He was being sucked deeper down into the murky depths of the muddy lake and there was little he could do to resist the pull.

There was no time to lose. Mr Muse put both hands on Bertie's shoulders and looked her square in the eyes.

"Listen very carefully and follow these instructions," he demanded. "In a moment you and I will appear in the lake next to your dad but we won't look like us. OK? I just need you to go with the flow. Are you with me on this?"

She knew this was not the time to entertain the idea of fear or nerves and she was almost giddy with a cocktail of anxiety and excitement.

"I'm with you. Just tell me what to do and I'll do it."

"Great. Right, climb onto my back and I'll start to carry you out into the lake. Now you must hold on tight as things are going to change, OK?"

"Yep," she said firmly as she jumped onto his broad back and hung onto his neck with her arms.

"Just go with the flow. And don't, whatever you do, call him Dad. Got it?"

"Got it," she affirmed.

"Let's go!" he cried and he stepped out into the shallow waters of the lake.

"Now, HOLD ON TIGHT!"

Bertie clung on to her companion's back as directed but he unexpectedly dropped to his knees and lowered his torso down until he was on all fours. She very nearly flew over the top of his head and was forced to tighten her grip around his neck, almost strangling the poor man. Then something most peculiar happened. Mr Muse began to change beneath her. His head grew larger and rounder and suddenly, two furry ears popped out. His shaggy mop of hair disappeared along with his pinstriped suite and in their place sprouted bright orange and black fur. Bertie felt her legs wrap around a large, soft belly and as she stretched out a tentative hand behind her, she felt more fur leading to a long swishy tail. She was indeed riding the big friendly tiger from the earlier dream. A smile lit her face as she stroked the silky fur. Her dad might be in danger but *she* was riding a tiger! Ha ha! This was so exhilarating she could hardly contain her excitement.

All smiles of delight were dispelled in an instant when Bertie heard more shocking screams from her dad. Transformation complete, the tiger dashed into the water and Bertie gripped the baggy fur around its neck as it swam rapidly towards her dad. Mr Brownlee was unaware of the approaching wild animal carrying his daughter at first and their sudden presence caused him great alarm. He thrashed his arms furiously in the water, trying in vain to scare the tiger away. Then he saw who was riding on its back.

"No! No!" he pleaded. "Don't hurt us. Please, don't hurt us!"

Bertie could see her dad was terrified, not only for his own safety but for hers too. She opened her mouth to speak but was completely taken aback by what came out.

"Don't be afraid, Darling, we're here to help you." The voice that emerged, rather alarmingly, was not hers. Looking down, Bertie discovered that her body wasn't hers either. The long brown hair around her shoulders didn't belong to her and the well-formed chest certainly wasn't hers. She had morphed into her mother. It felt very, very weird. Even stranger was Mr Muse's voice in her head.

"You have to grab him, Bertie – pull him out of the water." How did he do that? Was this telepathy?

"Quick, Bertie, before he goes under. If he does, it's likely to end his dream and he'll wake up!"

Bertie couldn't run the risk of getting stuck in her dad's dream, especially when she wasn't in her own body, so she plunged her arm into the dirty water and made a grab for her dad's hand.

"No, Bea!" spluttered Mr Brownlee as he splashed and kicked madly. "I'm being sucked down. If you grab my arm I'll take you down with me. It's not up to you to

137

save me. I should be strong enough to do this by myself."

"Don't be ridiculous, Brian!" shouted Bertie, her mouth working without her control. "We're in this together. We're a team - you're not on your own. Now for goodness sake take my hand."

"But the tiger…it'll get me," he panted.

"The tiger is here to help you," Bertie found herself saying. "We both are. Now please, take my hand."

Mr Brownlee had been fighting with all his might to resist the pull of the thick, deep muddy lake and it had taken all the strength he had to keep his face above the water but he was worn out by the struggle and he began to lose his breath. Finally, defeated by exhaustion, he gasped for air one last time then slipped slowly down below the surface.

Without a moment's hesitation, the tiger circled Mr Brownlee in the water and Bertie reached down to grab hold of her dad's hand. With surprisingly little effort, she pulled him free of the muddy water and hoisted him onto the tiger's back behind her. Within seconds, they were leaping out of the lake and back on dry land.

The heavy, dark feeling instantly lifted and the grey clouds dispersed revealing a clear blue sky. Mr Brownlee danced about, laughing with carefree abandon.

"Thank you, thank you, thank you, you've saved me," he cried as he hugged his wife and the tiger. But before Bertie could say anything, her dad fell into a trance, turned on his heels and began to run.

CHAPTER 19

"This isn't going to be easy to climb. I'm guessing that's what's coming next."

Bertie found herself at the foot of a snow-capped mountain, the tip of which was hidden in the clouds. "I'm so glad I've got my body back. Mum's would never be able to manage this."

"Now, Bertie," said Mr Muse scornfully, brushing two remaining whiskers from his cheeks. "Don't underestimate your mother's strengths. She did just rescue your father from certain doom."

"Technically, that was me," she said, cheekily as she looked for a sturdy rock to grab on to. "And talk about rude; I save Dad from drowning and he just runs off!"

"Welcome to my world," sighed Mr Muse. "I can't tell you how many times I've rescued people from disaster and they've just disappeared afterwards. Have you ever wondered why you never hit the ground in a falling dream? Because Dream Dwellers are always there to save people, that's why and we never get a word of thanks for it. Still," he sniffed. "It's the nature of the job."

The two of them embarked on their ascent of the rocky mountainside in pursuit of her dad as he continued on his epic journey to find his precious white car. As if battling fierce grizzly bears and nearly drowning in a muddy lake wasn't enough to wear him out, he'd now decided to take on a heroic climb. Bertie squinted her eyes to try and make out the top of the mountain.

"Surely he won't find his car up there."

Mr Muse held out a hand to aid her with the climb. "You seem to be forgetting you're in Dream World, anything can happen no matter how ridiculous."

"Should he not have woken up by now anyway?" she asked, reluctantly heaving herself up the rock face.

"He's on a roll tonight," chuckled Mr Muse, helping her with her footings in the rocks. "What did you make of what just happened? Did you understand why we morphed into your mother and the tiger?"

Stopping on a ledge to catch her breath, Bertie sat and thought for a while.

"I'm thinking it's because Mum said last night that she'll go back to work soon and help with the family finances. Plus she's always such a great support to my dad."

Mr Muse grinned at her. "She's going to take a greater role in helping your father than is evident at the moment. More than she could possibly realise herself actually."

"Hmmm...do you know how?" she enquired, suspiciously. Then she gasped in realisation. "You've worked it all out, haven't you?" Mr Muse said nothing but his broadening grin spoke volumes. "You have! You know what my dad's path is! Oh you have to tell me, Mr Muse, you have to."

"No, no, I can't tell you," he protested. "It wouldn't be right. A Dream Dweller never tells of his final intentions just in case they don't come to light."

"How do you mean?" she frowned.

"It's a bit like that phrase, 'you can lead a horse to water but you can't make it drink'. I can create lots of dreams or I can intercept and change dreams to show people their fate or destiny but it doesn't always mean they'll act on it. They may choose to totally ignore every message they receive and that's their choice, I can't control that. So you see, I don't want to tell you what your dad's destiny is in case he doesn't follow that path. I hope he does though as it could be...no, no, I shan't say anything else." He pulled an imaginary zip across his lips.

"So, who decides on a person's destiny, you or them?" Bertie asked, a little puzzled.

"Our fate and destiny are purely our own but many people are too scared to leave things to fate or to follow their destiny for fear of the unknown."

"And that's where you come in," Bertie added. "You give people messages or show them what they could achieve?"

"Sort of, yes, amongst many other things. For instance, take a look at this mountain, it looks impossible to climb doesn't it?"

"You're telling me! Especially in these shoes." She lifted her feet out in front to reveal her spectacularly sparkly black ballet pumps.

Mr Muse chuckled. "You know you can always change your clothing whenever it feels appropriate, I have told you that haven't I?"

"I know but I like them. We could never afford a pair of these back on earth so I'm going to wear them as much as I can, while I can." She took a moment to admire them. "Anyway, you were saying about this mountain."

"Yes, I was wasn't I. Well this mountain was one I created. Come on," he said clambering to his feet, "I want to show you something."

Cautiously, Bertie got to her feet and hung on to the rocks for dear life, not daring to look down.

"Can you see your father?" he asked. She looked a little way up the mountainside but her dad was nowhere to be seen. "He's not there," said Mr Muse.

Bertie looked at him searchingly. "Where is he then? Have we lost him?"

"No," he replied, "he's right up there."

Her eyes followed the direction of his pointed finger, way up in the snow and the clouds.

"How on earth did he manage that?" she cried in disbelief. "We've only been climbing for a short while."

"It turns out that what looked like a huge mountain to climb, was in fact as easy as walking up a small hill." A satisfied grin reached his lips and his eyes twinkled with mischief.

"It was easier to overcome this huge obstacle than he thought then," Bertie said, grinning back. "I'm liking your work, Mr Muse." The two of them giggled as they raced each other up the mountain, reaching the summit in seconds.

Once at the top they hid behind a boulder and watched Mr Brownlee as he assessed the scene that lay ahead of him. He was standing with his hands on his hips, shifting his gaze from left to right. He was no longer on top of the mountain but was instead, at the bottom of a lush green valley. To his left was a steep hillside with a small village perched on the top. Nothing but rows and rows of neat houses could be seen, each one identical to the next, all very understated and extremely dull. A huge grey cloud hung overhead, casting a shadow of gloom over the entire area. The village was dreary, boring and quiet, severely lacking in activity and atmosphere. Every drop of life had been cruelly sucked from its very foundations. Despite this, the village had a sense of safety and security.

Opposite this to his right was another steep hill. At its top, nestled neatly into the hillside, was an exciting little town full of bustling streets brimming with unique little shops and beautiful boutiques. People sat outside trendy cafes and classy restaurants, sipping wine and drinking frothy lattes. The glorious sun lit the faces of the townsfolk with bright smiles and the sound of merriment filled the air. Surrounding the town were exceedingly grand, white-bricked houses standing proud amongst plentiful fruit trees and carefully clipped gardens. Each home was different from the next; each one was a fantastically unique design.

Linking the two contrasting locations was a long, thin, winding tubular structure that began at the boring village on the left and snaked its way across the valley. It's many twists and turns at the start were followed by a sharp downward dip leading to a large U-shape before finally reaching up towards its destination of the exciting town on the right side.

Bertie had no idea what this tubular construction was but she had a sneaking suspicion she was about to find out as, in a split second, the three of them found themselves stood at the top of the left hill.

She felt a firm tap on her shoulder and turned to see a middle-aged gentleman in a black suit and tie, comedy moustache and black bowler hat.

"It's me," the strange man muttered from the side of his mouth, clearly not wanting to be overheard.

"Oh! Mr Muse!" Bertie gasped. "I didn't recognise you, sorry. You look very old fashioned."

"I think I look rather dashing myself," he joked, tweaking his moustache into little curls at each end. "Anyway, you don't look too clever yourself."

She glanced down at her legs and saw that she was wearing a neatly pleated brown A-line skirt and hideous beige court shoes.

"Oh dear, how very unstylish," she remarked. Mr Muse was sniggering like a little boy.

"You should see your hair, it's even worse."

Bertie put her hands to her hair and screwed up her nose in disgust as she felt short coiffured curls set tightly around her head.

Their attention was suddenly drawn to a large number of men and women all leaving their uniformed houses at the same time and who were heading their way. Weirdly, each and every one of them was dressed the same. The men were in sharp, black business suits and bowler hats and the women sported bland brown skirts, white blouses buttoned up to neck and a hairstyle that she had only ever seen on Queen Elizabeth II. Each wore a very sullen expression of gloom.

"Good grief, how odd," she proclaimed. What is all this about?"

Suddenly she spotted her dad in the forming crowd of clones. She could hardly miss him - he stood out like a poppy in a daisy field with his jeans and red t-shirt. But no one among the cloned crowd seemed to notice him. They were all on a mission to reach the mysterious tubular structure and they trudged, hypnotically towards it.

"We need to stick close to your father, Bertie," Mr Muse urged. "We can't afford to lose him. Follow me."

The pair jostled their way through the increasing crowd until they were right beside Mr Brownlee. Bertie wanted to laugh as she looked her Dad in the eye without even a flicker of recognition. She followed his gaze as he looked up towards a sign at the entrance of the tubular structure.

In bold green letters it read, 'Your Journey Starts Here.'

She stayed close to her dad in the packed crowd as it gradually edged forwards until finally they found themselves at the very front. It was here that the significance of the tubular structure was revealed. It was in fact a giant water slide - a great big theme park style water slide.

Mr Brownlee peered tentatively over the edge of the hill and observed the sheer scale of the drop. Bertie held her breath. She knew what a complete coward her dad was when it came to anything like this which was why they'd never visited a theme park in her life. Even the roundabout at the local play area was too much of a trial so there was no chance of him launching off the edge of this hill in a plastic tube.

Fear suddenly gripped him and he staggered backwards in a trembling, wobbly mess. Bertie reached out to steady him.

"Are you OK?" she dared ask. Her voice sounded strangely mature and womanly.

"I…I'm fine, thank you so much," he stammered. "I…I…I don't think I can do this though," and he turned to walk away.

"Wait!" she said firmly, stopping him in his tracks. "You can't give up now, you've come so far. Come on, you can do this. Yes, it's a big step but you'll never know what great things lay ahead unless you go for it. 'Fortune favours the brave' as they say. And just look at the reward."

Mr Brownlee peered over at the exciting town on the opposite hill then glanced back towards the boring village and the crowd of clones. He shook his head and rubbed his face with his hands.

"Ahhh!" he shouted. "I know I should do this but what if something goes wrong? What if I get stuck and don't make it to the other side? Then what?"

At his point, Mr Muse stepped forward. "Excuse me, sir," he announced in a frightfully posh voice. "I do hope you don't mind my interruption but I thought it might be helpful if perhaps you watched myself and this lady venture down the slide first, then you could see for yourself that it is perfectly safe. We shall wave to you from the other end to signal our safe arrival. How about that?"

"Yes," added Bertie, "I certainly wouldn't do anything that I regarded threatening or risky. I have a husband and two children to consider."

Mr Muse raised his eyebrows at her but she avoided eye contact with him for fear of the giggles. She rather enjoyed getting into character.

"OK," her dad sighed, heavily. "If you can do it, I'm sure I can."

With that, the three of them stood at the opening of the tubular slide next to a red stop light and waited. Bertie sat herself down in the gushing water ready to go and, as soon as the red light changed to flashing green, she launched herself off screaming.

"See you on the other siiiiiiiiiiiiiide. Wooohooooo!"

She flew off at great speed down the plastic pipe, the water washing her rapidly down, round, then round the other way.

"Woooohoooooo!" she screamed again as she was thrown this direction, then that, up the sides of the tube.

She weaved her way down into the valley, laughing with exhilaration all the way. The U turn approached out of the blue and she was plunged down the steep drop. It took her breath away and tickled her tummy, making her whoop involuntarily before being shot like a bullet back up the other side and blasted out of the exit in a gush of water and wild, excited screams.

High on the adrenalin, she clambered to her feet and jumped up and down, waving her arms about and shouting at the top of her lungs to her dad on the other hill.

"You've got to do it! It's amazing! Woooohoooo!"

Within minutes Mr Muse came crashing out of the slide with all the grace and elegance of a baby elephant and was welcomed by hysterical laughter as he splashed Bertie from head to toe.

"Wow! That really is an extreme ride. One of my best if I say so myself."

He rubbed the water from his eyes and tried to catch his breath. His bowler hat and nasty suit had disappeared and Bertie noticed that everyone who emerged on the other side had discarded their horrible business clothes and had reverted back to their regular ones. They were happy and smiling with utter relief and contentment. She reached her hand to her head and was pleased to feel her own hair once again. Phew. Thankfully the Queen hairstyle had vanished.

She turned her attention back to her dad at the top of the other hill.

"Do you think he's going to go for it then? What happens if he doesn't?" she asked her companion.

They gazed up at the hill and spotted Mr Brownlee standing at the opening of the slide. The green 'Go' light was visibly flashing yet he was hesitating.

"That hill represents all that is unfulfilling in his life. The drudgery and dullness of his job that he so despises. Obviously this hill represents the happiness that he could achieve if only he's brave enough to go ahead and follow the career path that is destined for him. He could be so happy and carefree here but he's scared that the journey will be a struggle and he won't succeed."

"And the slide represents the journey, right?"

"This dream is all about the journey."

"Oh, it's far from a struggle, it's the best fun I've had in my life," she declared. "It's so frustrating that you won't tell me what this career path is. I could encourage him to follow it."

"I will tell you this. Your father's journey to fulfilment will be fun and exciting for all of your family. But it's so very important that he discovers this for himself. If you were to tell him what it was, he wouldn't believe you anyway."

Her frustration levels rose even higher. This was as bad as being given big bowl of sweets with strict instructions not to eat them.

Just then they heard a man screaming hysterically. They looked back up at the hill to the slide entrance but there was no sign of Mr Brownlee. The screams could then be heard from inside the plastic slide and Bertie squeezed Mr Muse's arm in nervous anticipation.

"He's coming! He's done it!" she yelped dancing from one foot to the other. "He's on his journey."

Moments later, sure enough, Mr Brownlee came shooting out of the slide in a screaming heap, soaking everyone in sight. When he spotted his daughter he leapt to his feet and came bounding over. He flung his arms around her and lifted her high off her feet as he swung her around, laughing with euphoria and adrenalin.

"Bea! Billy!" he cried over her shoulder and before she knew it, she was engaged in a family hug. How strange it was to see everyone in her dad's dream.

As they all embraced, Bertie spotted Stella talking with Mr Muse. She wondered how long she'd been there - she hadn't noticed her before. Surely she would've come to say hello? Bertie gave her a little wave before closing her eyes to savour the joyous moment with her family. When she opened them again she found herself transported back to her street at home. Mr Muse was standing beside her and up ahead was her dad walking alone towards their house. Again, they followed him and as he reached their driveway he stood still, staring in disbelief. There, on the driveway was his precious, new, white car – just where he'd left it.

It had been there all this time. He just hadn't seen it.

CHAPTER 20

Bea Brownlee knocked quietly on her daughter's bedroom door and gently turned the handle to peep inside.

"Are you awake, Bertie?" she whispered.

Bertie slowly flipped her duvet back and sat up sleepily. "Hi Mum, what time is it?"

"It's just gone 7. I've come to see if you're alright, Love, you were screaming and shouting in your sleep just now."

"Was I?" she asked in surprise. The events of her Dream World adventures were still vivid in her mind and she smiled as she thought of the crazy water slide. Her Mum sat herself down on the bed next to her.

"It's been a strange morning. First you screamed and woke me up with a fright and then your dad started screaming his head off and thrashing about. I was really worried, I thought something terrible was happening."

"Did Dad say what he was dreaming about?" Bertie asked as casually as she could.

"Oh, something about a slide. Crazy fool."

"Who are you calling crazy?" Mr Brownlee appeared in the doorway all showered and dressed. "I'll have you know I was fighting off bears and climbing mountains last night."

Mrs Brownlee laughed. "I could understand it if you were screaming about fighting bears but you said it was a slide that made you scream – you big baby."

Bertie roared with laughter and her dad jumped on the bed to tickle her, making her wriggle and squeal.

"Oi you, Miss Bertie Brownlee, it was a massively high water slide and you know how I am with things like that. I was incredibly brave."

"Good for you, Dad," she said in between tickles, "I'm proud of you."

Bea huffed in exasperation. "He didn't *do* anything except scream and wake me up."

Dad picked up Bertie's pillow and swung it in his wife's face before leaping up and running away down the stairs.

"Where's he going in such a hurry?"

Mrs Brownlee straightened out her messed up hair. "To write his letter of resignation. He's going to tell Mr Hardwick today that he's quitting his job."

"What? Wow, he really means business then." Bertie did a victory dance in her head. The journey had begun. "How do you feel about all of this, Mum?"

Mrs Brownlee sighed. "It's got to be done hasn't it? I mean, it's not ideal but we've got to stay positive and as the saying goes, 'as one door closes another one opens'. I just hope it opens sooner rather than later."

"How can you *not* be positive when it's Christmas Eve tomorrow." Bertie got up and began jumping on her bed, "I'm so excited!"

Billy came running in and joined in with the bed bouncing.

"Santa's coming tomorrow night with aaaaalllllll my presents!" he yelled at the top of his lungs.

"Not if you break this bed he won't," shouted Mum. "Now get dressed."

That afternoon, Polly and TJ arrived at the house. The two women went off to the conservatory to finish their paintings for the Barnes charity fair and TJ and Bertie headed straight for the games room to begin writing the song for TJ's dad. Whilst the paintings came along brilliantly the song writing was less productive.

Despite their eagerness, Bertie and TJ were forced to admit that neither of them had written a song on their own before, and finding a catchy melody was far harder than they'd anticipated. They decided instead to work on some lyrics and this proved a little easier. After an hour or so, they'd written two verses and a simple chorus, which they chose to repeat rather than have to write more. They were really pleased with the words they had chosen but still the melody was not forth coming. TJ was feeling exasperated.

"We've only got tonight to do this. I can't see it happening, it's too hard. I'm beginning to understand what Dad meant about creative people being a bit mad – maybe they are driven mad by their lack of creativity."

Bertie wasn't giving up that easily. "Look, let's take a break and come back to this in a while. Mum will have dinner ready in a minute anyway and we can continue after that with fresh brains."

Dinner happened to be quite late due to Mrs Brownlee's usual painting frenzy, not to mention the glasses of wine she had consumed. It was a miracle that any food made it to the table at all. As everyone finished dessert, Mr Brownlee arrived home.

"Ah! Darling! Come and meet Polly and TJ," his wife called from the kitchen.

Mr Brownlee came in shivering from the sub-zero temperature outside and greeted the guests with a friendly yet freezing handshake.

"Hello! Lovely to meet you both." He studied Polly's face for a moment, squinting his eyes. "Have we met before? You look familiar."

"No, I don't think so," she replied rather awkwardly. "I must just have one of those faces."

"How was work, Darling?" asked Mrs Brownlee. "How did Mr Hardwick take the news of your resignation?"

"He was furious! He turned a different shade of purple that I've not seen before and then stormed out of the office for a few hours. If he could sack me tomorrow he would but he knows I'll sue him. Plus he needs me to finish this job."

"Oh dear," exclaimed Polly. "Trouble at work?"

"Brian handed his resignation in today," answered Mrs Brownlee before her husband had the chance. "His boss is an evil man-eating monster and he's not putting up with him any more are you, Dear? In fact, I think this is cause for a little celebration!" She promptly sloshed more wine into their glasses. Mr Brownlee shook his head.

"You two are tipsy aren't you?"

"We're just very happy, Darling. We finished our paintings today."

"We're celebrating," added Polly, raising her glass high in the air and giggling.

Bertie sensed her Dad's discomfort and seized the opportunity to whisk him off to help her. If she and TJ stood any chance of finishing their song tonight, they needed his experience and expertise.

After a quick dinner, Mr Brownlee happily trotted off to the sanity of the games room where Bertie and TJ confessed all about the song for TJ's dad. They'd wanted to keep it a secret but realised they had no choice.

"Do you think you can help us come up with a good melody?" TJ asked.

"I'd be delighted to," replied Mr Brownlee, happily. "You need to keep it simple though, so that people catch on to it quickly. Something like this…"

He sat himself down at the piano and started making up a tune. TJ's face lit up like an excited puppy.

"That's perfect, Mr Brownlee," he said. "Then it could go like this…" He picked up the tune on his guitar and added a catchy riff. In no time at all they had managed to fit an infectious melody to their perfectly penned lyrics. They ran through the song a few times, TJ on vocals and guitar, Mr Brownlee on piano and harmonies, and it sounded pretty amazing. But just when they thought the job was done, Mr Brownlee made a suggestion.

"Why don't you sing the backing vocals, Bertie. You should be part of this song too. It was your idea after all." Bertie shook her head and declined the offer.

"What's gotten into you, Bert? You love singing."

She shifted uncomfortably in her seat. "I do. I did. I don't really want to any more."

"What? Why not? You've got a beautiful voice. What's happened?" Her dad was stunned. He could never normally get Bertie to *stop* singing so this was hard for him to comprehend.

"Oh, it's just that, well, some girls said some horrible things about me after I sang at the nativity and it's made me self conscious now. I wasn't going to sing in front of anyone ever again."

Her dad was mortified. "You never said anything, Darling. Besides, your mum said you'd moved everyone to tears your voice was that beautiful. Who were these girls?"

"Just some girls in my class. I don't have much to do with them really, they're a bit, well, cool and I'm not.

"They're jealous," said TJ, indignantly. "Jealous, nasty girls who wish they had half your talent and beauty. Isn't that right, Mr B?"

"Absolutely!" cried her dad. "Girls like that are not worth the time of day."

"Don't you dare let them stop you singing, Bertie Brownlee!" shouted TJ in his best British accent. "Come on, get up and grab this mic. You will not be silenced by jealousy; I won't have it. Never let anyone steal your sparkle."

"Here, here," agreed her dad.

"In fact," TJ said, "sing the lead. Sing it all and sing it proud."

Bertie threw her head back and laughed as she took the mic. Somehow she had a feeling that neither of them would say anything nasty even if she sounded like a horse with a sore throat.

As soon as she began to sing, she felt she'd come home. This was the most natural thing in the world to her and she'd missed it dearly.

"WOW! Your voice is awesome. It's so pure and angelic. Man, you have to sing this at the party, you're miles better than me." TJ was staring at Bertie in awe and she didn't know what to do with her face. Compliments always made her feel so uncomfortable and she was suddenly very aware of her limbs – were they always this long? And where did she usually put her arms? She found herself agreeing to his demands just to make the awkwardness stop. In an attempt to divert the attention away from herself, she promptly grabbed the Stratocaster and plugged it in.

"Talking of good, here, you should play something for Dad, TJ. Show him how talented *you* are."

TJ didn't need to be asked twice. He totally rocked out, blasting their eardrums with the finest guitar solos he knew. Then he surprised them by toning it right down and playing sweet, melodic songs that required lightening speed fingering on the frets and strings. When he'd finished, his audience of two gave him a standing ovation with whistles and cheers.

157

"You are some guitarist!" gushed Mr Brownlee. "That guitar solo is going into the song. When your dad hears this he is going to be blown away! How could he not be proud of you, TJ? You're the same age as Bertie and you can play like that? Wow!"

"I'm slightly older actually but thank you," TJ mumbled as he ruffled his hair. He wasn't good with compliments either.

"Dad wishes he could play as well as you." Bertie loved winding him up.

"Actually, I'm a very accomplished player," he declared, grabbing the guitar from TJ and bursting into a mad guitar riff of his own. He began prancing around causing Bertie to shake her head in shame.

"He thinks he's Tiger Jonz," she snorted.

TJ let out a loud laugh. "You like Tiger Jonz?! That's hilarious."

Mr Brownlee suddenly stopped playing. He couldn't believe TJ's reaction. "Is that a such a bad thing? The man's an absolute legend. His guitar playing is second to none and his songs are timeless, don't you agree?"

TJ shook his head resignedly. "Yeah, I guess so."

"Sorry, TJ, Dad's a massive fan. You can't diss The Tiger."

"I didn't mean to offend you, Mr Brownlee," TJ said earnestly, "I'm very sorry. Anyway, thanks a million for helping us write the song. I think he…my dad that is, might really like it. It would mean so much to me if he accepted my love for music."

"You're very welcome, son," said Mr Brownlee with a soft smile. "It's been a great pleasure; I've really enjoyed tonight. It's ages since I've written any songs and I'd quite forgotten how good it feels."

"Well you're very good." TJ threw him a cheeky smile. "Almost as good as Tiger Jonz!"

CHAPTER 21

Long after Polly and TJ had left and the family had gone to bed, Brian Brownlee stayed up playing his guitar and singing in the games room. He'd been there so long he'd left very little time for dreaming and this meant that Bertie and Mr Muse had their work cut out.

"We've got a lot to do in a very short space of time tonight," announced Mr Muse upon Bertie's arrival in Dream World. "It's vital that we get your dad to realise his destiny and to do that I'm going to recreate an old recurring dream."

"Right O," said Bertie, securing the buttons on her red, fur-trimmed coat. "To be honest I'm so very excited about Christmas Eve tomorrow that I'm buzzing tonight and up for any challenges that come our way. Bring it on."

"Only one day to go, then you'll be in Christmas heaven." Mr Muse watched as Bertie stared at her Morpheus statue creating the Gateway.

"I know!" she squeaked, rubbing her hands together. "I can't wait. Come on, let's give Dad the best Christmas present ever," and with that, the pair jumped through the glowing circle of light into the dream dimension.

Bertie was prepared for the blinding flash of light this time and when she opened her eyes she found herself on a railway platform awaiting a train. It was a single platform in an isolated spot in the middle of nowhere. There were no visible houses or towns nearby, not even grass or fields, just the platform and the train track. A large number of people stood waiting with them but no one spoke and no eye contact was made. Similar to some of his previous dreams, this too was all very dreary and slightly depressing. The mood totally deflated Bertie's Christmas hysteria.

"Oh," she said flatly. "This isn't quite what I was expecting. How dull."

Mr Muse looked her up and down and sniffed. "You're clothes aren't dull today though are they?"

Bertie looked about her person and laughed aloud. "Goodness, what have you done to me this time?" She was wearing an all-in-one bright pink rabbit outfit complete with long floppy ears and, oh yes, a round fluffy white tail.

"Actually, you have to blame your dad for that," Mr Muse stated. "I've created this dream but it's his mind that has filled it with whatever is going on in his head. Totally random stuff isn't it?"

Bertie looked more closely at the other people on the platform. Amongst the oddly dressed passengers was a seven-foot tall man and a woman who was wearing a pair of oversized wooden clogs. Mr Muse had come out of this relatively unscathed as he was dressed in an almost respectable green tweed suit but on his feet were a pair of women's delicate, silver, strappy high heeled sandals complete with pretty diamonds across the toes. Bertie sniggered. He scowled back at her.

"Button it, Bunny!"

161

Further along the platform was her dad. He was dressed in his work suit and was repeatedly checking his watch as he paced up and down.

"So what is going on anyway, is there a train coming?" Bertie asked.

"Well, that's up to your dad. I've gone for the classic 'train dream'. The objective is for him to board the train and arrive at his destination where he will discover his destiny. I've created this dream for your father many times over the years for varying reasons, as it's a good one for finding solutions to problems. Thing is, each time he's come up with something different. Either he's waiting for a train and it doesn't come, or the train comes and, for some reason he can't get on it. Quite often he keeps missing the trains that pass through the station and sometimes he manages to board the train but it doesn't move. It's stuck and it's going nowhere."

"So what will it look like, this destiny?"

Mr Muse cleared his throat and shuffled from one foot to the other. Those heels were killing his feet.

"We probably won't see it, in fact we don't need to see it. We'll just *know* when it happens. We'll be able to feel it, you know? He'll get off the train and be 'there'."

"Great, sounds simple."

"It does, doesn't it? Except after years of this recurring dream he has only got as far as getting on the train once. I just thought I'd try it again as we are so close to him discovering his new career path that he might manage to reach his destiny tonight. He's handed in his resignation at work and that shows that last nights dreams were a success; he's taken the plunge and is on his journey already. This is the last piece of the puzzle now. It's got to be worth a try."

"Hey!" said Bertie, giving her companion's arm a prod, "a train is coming." They watched as it slowed down to a stop beside the platform. The two of them casually made their way over to Mr Brownlee and stayed close to his side. He didn't even notice Bertie's pink bunniness or the strange man tottering about in women's heels next to him.

The train doors directly in front of them slid open. The three of them were about to board when there was a sudden rush of people. All of the other doors to the train had jammed shut, forcing everyone from the platform to dash over and try to bundle onto the train through this one open section. A lot of elbowing and pushing ensued and panic set in. Desperation to board the train had created heightened tension amongst the passengers and a small scuffle broke out to their right. The seven-foot man had barged his way to the front and taken up the entire door space with his giant body, causing everyone to hurl abuse at him. Then the woman with the oversized clogs followed him and took forever to step into the train. The passengers lost their patience and began to shove the poor woman forwards until she fell headfirst into the carriage, leaving her massive clogs on the platform for everyone to stumble over.

"Oh my goodness!" Bertie gasped "What a nightmare. No wonder Dad never gets on the train."

Mr Muse whispered in Bertie's ear so Mr Brownlee couldn't over hear. "He keeps putting obstacles in his way. These are all things to stop him from getting where he needs to be. Reasons not to get there. Fear of the unknown."

Bertie thought for a second and then took action.

"Look!" she cried, "those doors have opened up there. Quick!"

Without looking, the passengers took off up the platform, budging each other out of the way as they ran, frantically searching for the open train doors. Bertie winked at Mr Muse and they quickly hustled forward onto the train, sweeping her dad along with them.

"Beep, beep, beep, beep, beep, beep, beep," went the doors as they slammed shut immediately behind them. The three of them fell into the seats and as the train pulled away from the platform, the angry stranded passengers banged on the windows and shook their fists at Bertie.

"Naughty Bunny," said Mr Muse, tutting and shaking his head. "But very clever Bunny too."

The train rattled on for what seemed like an eternity despite only seconds passing. Bertie peered out of the windows but all she saw was a coloured blur. After previous nights of high drama and action, this dream was deathly dull and intensely boring. Her dad sat motionless, staring straight ahead.

Bertie leaned in and whispered in her companion's ear.

"What's Dad doing just sitting there?"

"He's thinking," he whispered back.

"About what?"

"What his next job should be and what he should do with his life." Mr Muse was perched on the edge of his seat looking nervously around. For the first time since she'd met him, Bertie found him a bit fretful and tense. It was very unlike him. She didn't give it too much thought though, as she was busy wriggling about. She couldn't find a way to sit comfortably with a large round fluffy tail on her bottom.

"If he realises what it is, does that mean we can get off this awful train?" she huffed.

"Are you actually going to ask me if we're nearly there yet?" he said, raising an eyebrow.

"No I'm not," she snapped. "But you've got to admit, this is very boring."

"It's necessary though. If he can come to his own conclusion then we've cracked it. He just needs time, although we really don't have much of that left."

At that moment they heard a familiar sound.

Beep, beep, beep, beep, beep, beep, beep.

"It's the doors, the doors are opening. We must be here!" Bertie yelled, excitedly. She leapt out of her seat and dashed for the exit.

"No! Bertie, it's not the doors," shouted Mr Muse tottering after her in his ridiculous silver heels. "You must come with me. Quickly, take my hand, we've got to go!"

Bertie pushed madly on the doors but they wouldn't open. The beeping continued. She became anxious that they wouldn't get off the train in time. She began to panic and bunny hopped off up the carriage to the next set of doors to try those instead.

"Come on, Dad!" she yelled. "Follow me, we've got to get off. You're here."

"No, Bertie!" Mr Muse tried desperately to run up the train aisle after her but his high heels got the better of him and his right ankle buckled. He fell to the floor of the train screaming at the top of his voice, "Bertie! We're not here. Stop! Please, you have to come with me, NOW." He scrambled to his knees and attempted to stand, not realising one of the heels on his strappy shoes had snapped. He tumbled to the floor again. "*Now*, Bertie. Quick!"

But Bertie didn't look back. She didn't listen to her companion's pleas, nor did she come to his aid. She was on a mission to save her dad and nothing was going to stop her. Still, the beep, beep, beep of the train doors sounded in her ears.

"Bertie, come with me NOW! screamed Mr Muse. But his cries fell on deaf ears.

"Dad! Come on, please, Dad, get off the train! Please, Dad!" she pleaded.

Beep, beep, beep, beep went the doors again.

Then, BOOOOOFF!

Everything stopped.

Beep, beep, beep, beep, beep....

"Brian, Brian! Wake up. You're alarm clock has been going off for ages. I'm not hitting the snooze button again."

Mr Brownlee awoke with a start and stretched out his arm. He reached over and turned off the alarm.

Everything had gone quiet. All Bertie could hear was the rumble and rattle of the train as it trundled along the track to - she knew not where. She looked around. The seven-foot man, the cloggless woman and a number of other strange looking passengers were all staring into space, suspended in animation. Mr Muse and her dad had disappeared. She was, it would seem - stuck.

CHAPTER 22

Billy came charging into his parent's bedroom in an arm waving frenzy of excitement.

"Mummy, Daddy, it's Christmas Eve and look! Look outside, quick!"

Mr Brownlee clambered out of bed, pulled opened the bedroom curtains and found the whole of Barnes had been hidden under a thick blanket of snow. Everywhere was completely white.

"Man! Where did that lot come from? That wasn't there when I went to sleep last night. Come and look, Bea."

Mrs Brownlee struggled out of bed and trudged wearily over to the window. "Wow, that *is* a lot of snow. There must have been a blizzard in the night. Billy, go and wake your sister, she's going to be hysterical when she sees this."

Billy disappeared off yelling, "snow, snow! Bertie wake up there's snow. Let's make a snowman."

Being the ever practical grown up, Mrs Brownlee's attention turned to her husbands safety.

"Darling, I don't think you should go into work today, it's too dangerous to drive. Besides, the car is practically buried under a snow drift." She was right, the wind had blown the snow up against their car and only the top half of the vehicle was visible.

"I'll have to take the bus," he said. "Mr Hardwick will only accept 'death' as an excuse not to make it into work so a bit of snow is not a satisfactory reason to be absent. Anyway I can't miss today because the evil man needs to pay me my Christmas cash bonus. We need every penny we can get if I'm going to be out of work in a months time."

His wife tried desperately to stop him venturing out so early in the extreme weather. She was quite sure there wouldn't be any buses running anyway but there was no arguing with him. He was showered, dressed, breakfasted and off up to the bus stop before Bertie had even woken up. But then, that was the problem.

She hadn't woken up.

She couldn't wake up.

"Mummy, Bertie is still asleep," hollered Billy for the tenth time that morning.

"I know, Sweetheart," came Mum's tenth reply. "She must just be really tired. Let her sleep, she obviously needs it."

After some time, Mrs Brownlee began to find it odd that her daughter had slept through Billy's shouting for so long and she ventured up to her room to see if she could wake her.

"Bertie. Bertie. It's Christmas Eve and it's been snowing," she said, giving her arm a gentle shake.

Bertie didn't flinch. She didn't even flutter her eyelids. "Fine," sighed Mum, a little bemused. She had been expecting her daughter to wake the whole house up before any alarms that morning, given what day it was. "You're missing out on precious hours of one of your favourite days of the year!" Still no response. After a while, she gave up trying and closed the door to let her daughter sleep.

Meanwhile, the train rattled on and on.

And on, and on, and on and on.

Bertie was beside herself with fear and dread. She paced up and down the train trying to make sense of what had just happened. What had she done? Why hadn't she paid attention to Mr Muse? He'd said to stay close to him and she hadn't listened. This was all her fault and she knew it.

She sat down next to a passenger with green hair and a false beard and proceeded to talk at him.

"It's Christmas Eve today you know. *Christmas Eve*!

"This is the time of year that I look forward to all year round. *All year round*!"

The man continued to stare into space.

"Not that you care. You're not even real, are you? You're just some weird figment of my dad's warped imagination. But *I* care. I care a lot actually."

She quite liked the fact that the green haired man was suspended in the dream and incapable of responding. She didn't feel so guilty offloading on him like this. In fact it was quite liberating. At least he couldn't laugh at her pink bunny outfit.

"I'm probably not going to wake up until tonight now when my dad goes back to sleep and I'll have missed the *whole* of Christmas Eve. I'll have missed badly decorating Mum's Christmas cake with my dad. I'll have missed carols around the tree before bed and most of all I will have missed the Christmas Fair where I was going to help my friend mend his broken relationship with his father.

"And do you know what? Do you know what the worse thing is, Mr Green Man? No? I'll tell you. I will wake up tonight. *Tonight*! And, I'll be awake *all* night because I will have been asleep *all day*. Now *that* is not good my friend, not good at all because I will then be tired on Christmas Day – THE MOST IMPORTANT DAY OF THE YEAR AND I WILL BE HALF ASLEEP! This is the worst day of my life."

And with that, Bertie put her head in her hands and sobbed.

CHAPTER 23

Despite the arctic temperature and the stupidly early start to this festive day, Mr Brownlee thoroughly enjoyed his brief walk to the bus stop that morning. No one else was about so he had the entire village to himself. He was the first to make a mark on the blank canvas of pure white snow and he leapt, childlike across the green, giving in to the temptation to make a quick snowman. He threw snowballs at the trees and dodged the ensuing avalanche from the branches above his head. The pond had frozen over and he laughed aloud as he watched a duck skate clumsily across it, slipping at every comedy step. This was such a magical place, he thought, but never more so than when it had been 'touched by the Snow Queen', as Bertie would put it.

He began to feel a twinge of excitement about that afternoon. The office was closing at 4pm and he was going to dash home in time for the end of the Christmas Fair and just in time for the live music and dancing. He was going to enjoy his one day off with his family more than any holiday he'd ever had.

After over half an hour of waiting at the bus stop, he was no longer able to feel his toes. In his rush to leave for London, he hadn't packed his snow boots or his thick winter puffer coat so he'd had to wear his little bomber jacket and a pair of Mr Muse's wellington boots - and everyone knows that wellies are freezing in the snow.

A few people had gathered at the bus stop by now and they'd started a conversation about whether the roads were clear enough for the buses to get through. A lady in a full snow suit and a Russian hat seemed to take control of the group and suggested they walk up to the main road at the top of the village to see if the buses were running better from there. He followed the group as they snaked their way through the deep snow up the road. To his surprise he walked past a recording studio on his left hand side. How did he not know that was there? He recognised the name, 'Nassau Studios'; it was where many great artists had recorded legendary albums. The revelation lifted his spirits. He was living in the presence of rock coolness and he hadn't even realised. This helped to put a spring in his frozen step.

An hour had passed since leaving the house by the time he'd reached the main road. Mr Hardwick was already calling Mr Brownlee's mobile, demanding to know where he was. He tried explaining that the buses weren't running but that sent Mr Hardwick into one of his ranty rages and Mr Brownlee had to pretend to lose signal and cut him off.

After a while the main road had cleared a little by the traffic passing through and eventually a bus came along. Everyone cheered as it approached and then booed as the bus trundled straight past with the squashed up faces of too many passengers crammed on board. Several more buses approached and zoomed past in a similar fashion before one finally arrived with space for the poor frozen people. Two hours after leaving his house, Mr Brownlee was finally on his way.

He sat shivering in his seat with his teeth chattering loudly. The cold had penetrated right through to his bones. He wondered if he might lose a couple of fingers to frostbite. He'd seen it happen to those explorers. He did hope not, but then again, it would be a good excuse not to call his boss back.

Bertie had stopped sobbing and her tears had turned to resentment. She'd moved on from the green haired man with the false beard and was now venting her depression on a pregnant businessman, reading his newspaper. She knew she was as annoying as a drunk uncle at a wedding, but she didn't care.

"Of all the dreams my dad has had this week, I have to get stuck in *this* one. Why couldn't Mr Muse have thought up a more exciting dream to take Dad to his destiny? Huh? I mean, trains! They're not the most exciting mode of transport in the world. This one doesn't even have a trolley service for goodness sake. And to make things worse, I'm dressed as a bright pink bunny. Great. Just great.

"If I'd got stuck in the dream with the water slide then well, I wouldn't be complaining, would I? At least I'd have been having fun until Dad woke up. But no, I'm stuck on a train going goodness knows where with goodness knows who for goodness knows how long – for goodness sake!

"This isn't Dream World, this is hell!"

Brian Brownlee's teeth were still chattering and his fingers and toes had gone from frozen to down right painful (but thankfully still attached to his body). The bus had covered the majority of the journey to Richmond fairly well, considering the slippery snow and icy roads, but just when it looked as though they'd make their journey in fairly good time, the bus made a sudden strange "splurg, splurg, splurge, clonk" sound and came to an abrupt stop at the bottom of a small hill.

The driver jumped out to inspect his vehicle, then jumped back on to make the unwelcome announcement that the bus had broken down. There was a collective groan from the passengers and one by one they reluctantly disembarked. Seemingly just on cue, snow had started to fall heavily as Mr Brownlee began to trudge up the hill towards his office. He knew it wouldn't be long before Mr Hardwick was back on the warpath and sure enough, as predicted, his phone rang in his pocket.

"Mr Hardwick the bus just broke down so I'll be there as soon as I can," he panted wearily. "I'm walking up the hill now."

"You're pushing your luck, Brownlee. If you don't get here in 10 minutes you can kiss goodbye to your Christmas cash bonus. Is that clear?"

If it wasn't for the fact that the family needed that bonus, he would have given up on this arduous journey long ago. He'd arranged for them all to have Christmas dinner at the local restaurant as a special treat tomorrow and he wouldn't be able to afford it without the bonus.

Plus, they hadn't got a turkey to cook for Christmas dinner at home so they *had* to go to the restaurant. He *had* to get to work. But this was the last time he'd put himself through anything like this for the sake of some rubbish job and some stupid angry little man. This was the final straw. Things were going to change; he was going to make sure of it.

Bertie had now given up talking to weird looking, non-responsive people and had returned to sobbing into her hands. She had no idea how long she'd been stuck on this godforsaken train and she had no idea how much longer she'd be there. She remembered what Stella had said about there being no sense of time in Dream World and she hoped this meant she'd been there for many hours but similarly, it could've meant that she'd only been there for a few minutes.

So many disturbing thoughts tore through her mind. What if her parents had got so worried about her not waking up that they'd called an ambulance? What if she'd been taken to hospital and had to wake up there on Christmas Day? How would she convince the doctors that she was ok and that she hadn't been in some kind of coma? Would they let her go home or would she have to stay in over Christmas? The more she thought about this, the more she worried and the more she worried, the more desperate she became. This was by far the worst thing that had ever happened to her. She curled up on the hard seats and wept uncontrollably.

The snow was coming down thick and fast now, soaking through his inadequate clothing and punishing his already frozen skin. His toes were now so painful that he winced with every tiny step he took, inching so, so slowly up the hill. Weeks of overwork and too little sleep were beginning to take their toll and his tired body grew feeble. His legs had turned to jelly and his breath was rasping and laboured but he was determined to get to the office. He had to. He heaved his weary body on and on, hardly noticing that he was staggering from one side of the path to the other. It was then that his head began to spin and his vision blurred. He blinked hard and shook his head, staggering this way, then that until finally, he could go on no further.

Bertie wasn't sure what made her look up from her sobs but something had caught her eye and it gave her a start. There, sat right in front of her was her dad. He'd come back.

"Dad!" she screamed at him. She had to think quickly. Should she try and launch herself upwards and out of the dream back to the safety of her D-zone or should she try and help her dad off the train so that he reached his destiny? She knew the safe thing to do was leave the dream but she didn't even know how. Where was Mr Muse?

Left with no other choice she sat down next to her dad and took his arm. She knew she had to act fast.

"Dad! Dad! I don't know if you can hear me but I want you to know this. Whatever your dream is, go for it. Please, Dad, don't be afraid, just take the plunge yeah? Don't worry about anything because we'll be ok, all of us. We'll be great, as long as you follow your heart and do what you need to do."

Her dad seemed to listen but he didn't respond. Bertie's heart was racing so fast she could hear her heartbeat in her ears. How much time did she have? She was torn between the risk of getting stuck again and not wanting the torture of this awful train dream to have been in vein.

"Please, Dad, go for it. *Please!*" she begged.

"Bertie, you 'ave to come with me now girl!" demanded a man's voice from behind her. "Quick, take me 'and." She spun around and looked up to a familiar dark craggy face with sparkly gem stone eyes.

"Curtis! It's you!"

"I've been waiting to rescue you," he said, urgently. "Come on, let's go."

She took one last look at her dad before she grabbed onto Curtis' hand and was flown skywards, back through the dream dimension and out through the Gateway into the garden of her D-zone.

"We did it girl! We got you 'ome safe."

"Curtis," puffed Bertie, "What are you doing here?"

Curtis sat himself down on a bench in her warm snowy garden and mopped his forehead.

"You gave an ol' man a fright ya know, little lady," and he let out one of his raucous laughs. "Mr Muse sent me. I've been waiting to jump through your Gateway the minute your dad appeared so I could rescue you. Mr Muse sends his apologies for what 'appened last night and he's sorry he couldn't be 'ere to rescue you because he's on urgent business. I'm on American time so I was happy to help."

"Oh Curtis, I'm so happy to see you, thank you so much for rescuing me."

"Ah now girl," he roared, "That's what I'm 'ere for, to 'elp people."

Bertie felt that strange sensation again as if she was being pulled backwards and she knew she was fading.

"I've got to go, Curtis, I'm waking up. Thank you so much. Goodbye!"

"See you tonight at the party," he called after her and, in a flash, she was gone.

CHAPTER 24

Upon opening her eyes, Bertie was shocked to find daylight filling her room. She sat bolt upright as a stream of frightening thoughts ripped through her mind. Her dad would've been at work on Christmas Eve and there was no way he would've been asleep during the day. So, if it was daylight now, then she must have slept for the whole of Christmas Eve and all of that night too. Therefore, it must be… Christmas Day!

"Oh my goodness, I've missed Christmas Eve!" she said aloud. "Oh no! I can't have missed it, I can't have."

She panicked and stumbled out of bed. If this was Christmas Day, she didn't want to miss a single precious moment. As she threw on her dressing gown and pulled on her fluffy slippers she was struck with guilt. TJ! What happened about his song? Had he performed it himself? She'd really let him down and she felt awful. Everything had gone so disastrously wrong.

She tore down the stairs and dashed into the kitchen to find her mum taking her Christmas cake out of the oven.

"Ah, Bertie. Crikey, you've had a long sleep, Love. Are you ok?"

Bertie stood staring at her mum. She couldn't work out why she was making the cake on Christmas Day, she always made it on Christmas Eve. And if Bertie had been in bed for about 34 hours, why was her mum so calm about it?

"Bertie, Love, are you alright, you look a bit pale. Shall I put some toast on for you?"

"Mum, what time is it?" she asked in a daze.

"It's getting on for 10.30, Darling. You've never slept in this long in your life. I'd have thought you'd be up at the crack on Christmas Eve."

"Christmas *Eve*?! It's Christmas *Eve*, not Christmas *Day*?"

Mrs Brownlee stopped what she was doing and went over to her daughter. "Darling, you're not ok are you? I knew there was something wrong when I couldn't wake you. Come here, let me check your temperature."

"No, Mum I'm fine," Bertie protested, gently batting her mum's hand away from her brow. She flopped into a chair and breathed a huge sigh of relief. "Oh thank goodness I haven't missed anything." Her mum gave her a worried look and went to look for her thermometer.

"Mum, seriously I'm fine. It's just that, well, I had this really vivid dream last night that I'd slept through Christmas Eve so when I woke up I was convinced it was Christmas Day. I can't tell you how relieved I am."

"Oh Darling," said Mum stroking her daughter's hair, "that's horrible, especially for a Christmas fairy like yourself. Well, it's very much Christmas Eve and I've got lots to do if we're going to make it to this fair later. Hurry up and eat your breakfast and then you can join Billy outside in the snow. There'll be none left if you..."

"SNOW?!" Bertie looked out of the patio doors to see Barry jumping about trying to catch snowflakes and Billy building a snowman far bigger than himself.

"Good grief, Bertie, how could you not have noticed how white it is outside?"

Things began to make a bit of sense now.

"So is Dad still in bed then? He can't have gone to work in this?" she asked. That would explain why he'd fallen asleep and released her from the nightmare train dream.

"Can you believe it, that stupid father of yours insisted on getting the bus into work because the car was snowed in. Goodness knows how long it will have taken. I'm a bit concerned that he'll get stranded though because it hasn't stopped snowing since about 9 o'clock. Oh, wouldn't it be awful if he was stranded there and had to spend Christmas with The Evil Mr Hardwick in those new offices," she laughed.

So the mystery of why her dad had fallen asleep in the middle of the morning remained and she still didn't know if he'd reached his destination in the dream either but she didn't dwell on it too much. She was sure there was a perfectly reasonable explanation. Besides, she had snowmen to build.

Once washed and dressed, she put her shoes on and ran out into the snowy garden. Her feet froze in an instant; she'd completely forgotten that real snow was not warm or dry. There had hardly been time to change into her wellies and throw snowballs at her brother when the doorbell rang. She assumed it would be TJ - he'd probably wanted someone to play in the snow with. She went inside and into the hallway where she found her mum opening the front door to a shivering, wet Dad.

"Brian, whatever's happened to you!" cried Mum in distress. There stood Mr Brownlee in a very sorry state, hardly able to speak. Standing on the doorstep behind him was a young gentleman.

"Hello there," said the young man, a little awkwardly. "Errrm…I was driving from Richmond and I saw your husband lying on the pavement on the other side of the road so I stopped to see if he was alright. He'd passed out in the snow. He quickly came round though, so I don't think he'd been out for long and he seems OK."

"Oh!" cried Bertie – more in realisation rather than concern.

"Oh my Goodness, Brian, I told you not to go out in this weather. You're frozen right through. Quick, quick! Come in and get warm." Mrs Brownlee pulled her husband into the hallway and hugged him tightly.

The young gentleman watched for a moment, then stepped backwards off the doorstep and walked briskly back up the drive calling behind him.

"I'll be going then. I hope you feel better soon."

"Thank you so much," Mrs Brownlee called after him, a little flustered. She'd wanted to invite him in to thank him properly but he was already gone.

"I tried my hardest to get to work, Bea, I really did," whispered Mr Brownlee, weakly. "Mr Hardwick rang several times this morning telling me that I wouldn't get the bonus if I didn't make it in."

"Sod the bonus!" snapped Mum. "Look what that bloomin' horrible man has done to you. It's snowing for goodness sake, how can he expect people to get to work in this weather." She sat him down on the stairs and he winced in pain as she helped him off with his wellington boots.

Mr Brownlee relayed the story of events leading up to the bus breaking down and his attempt to walk the rest of the way to the office.

"I feel such an idiot, I couldn't even walk up a small hill."

"Darling, you're exhausted, you've been working ridiculously long hours lately, what do you expect."

Mr Brownlee's phone began to ring in his coat pocket. "That'll be him again," he sighed.

"Give me that!" Before he could stop her, his wife had grabbed the phone and was pressing the green answer button.

"BROWNLEE? WHERE THE DEVIL ARE YOU?" came the booming voice at the other end. "This is your final warning. I'm giving you an extra 5 minutes and if you're not here you can forget about that bonus!"

"This is *Mrs* Brownlee," said Mum in a calm and unusually assertive voice.

"Oh! Errr…Mrs Brownlee, hello, how are you?" Mr Hardwick stammered. He sounded like a little boy who'd been caught stealing sweets.

"Mr Hardwick, you horrible little man," she spat. Bertie and her dad gawped in shock. It was so out of character for this mild mannered woman to be so rude. "My husband has done nothing but work his butt off for your company all these years. I told him not to go into work this morning because it was too dangerous but he insisted. In fact, he's been trying since 7.30 to make it into the office. Now, it might interest you to know that he's just been brought home by a complete stranger who came to his rescue because he'd passed out in the street due to hypothermia. And after all that, you have the nerve to tell him, on *Christmas Eve*, that he won't get his bonus? What's your middle name, Scrooge? Now you listen to me, you monster, you can shove that bonus where the sun doesn't shine and what's more, you can shove your stupid job there too. Don't you *ever* call this phone again or I will call the police and have you done for harassment. IS THAT CLEAR?!" And with that, she hung up. "Right, that's sorted then." She casually handed the phone back to her husband.

There was a stunned silence while Mr Brownlee tried to compute what had just happened. Then, much to Bertie's surprise, he burst out laughing.

He laughed and laughed.

He laughed so much he didn't think he would stop.

He laughed until he made wife and daughter laugh too.

When he finally pulled himself together, he raised his arms in the air and limped around the hall shouting, "I'm free! Free at last! Free from The Evil Man-eating Mr Hardwick and his stupid computers. No more boring work."

"So you're not cross with me then?" his wife asked with a sheepish grin. "We needed that bonus to pay for our Christmas dinner tomorrow and now we haven't got enough money to buy a turkey or do a food shop."

"Cross? Good God no! I've been wanting to tell him to stick his job for years. Besides, we don't need money to make us happy, we've got each other. I'll cancel the restaurant - I'm happy with beans on toast for Christmas dinner. We can have turkey any time."

Billy came running in to see his dad, leaving little puddles of melting snow as he went. Mr Brownlee hugged his children and kissed them both on the cheek.

"Now I get to totally relax and spend the whole of Christmas with my wonderful family. This is the best Christmas present I could possibly wish for. Everything will turn out just fine, you wait and see."

"I'll run you a bath to warm you up, Dad, you're still frozen," said Bertie feeling her dad's cold hands on her face.

She darted up the stairs into the bathroom and turned on the taps. Then she stared at her reflection in the bathroom mirror. What had she done? This wasn't how things were meant to end. Up until now everything had gone according to plan but it was supposed to conclude with her dad finding fulfilment in the shape of an exciting new job. Instead she'd steered him in the direction of unemployment and no money. On top of that, she'd made him believe that everything would be ok. But right now, it was far from ok. And it was all her fault.

CHAPTER 25

Mr Brownlee was about to climb into his warm bath and defrost when he heard a heavy lorry pulling up their gravel drive. The doorbell rang and his wife went to answer it. There on the doorstep stood a man from an extremely high-end, hugely expensive food store.

"Good morning, madam," said the very polite gentleman. "I'm from Henleigh and McVey Fine Foods. I have a food order for you."

Before Mrs Brownlee could say anything, his colleagues proceeded to unload six large pale blue and gold boxes into the hallway of the house while he produced a clipboard.

"If you wouldn't mind signing here, madam," he smiled, offering Mrs Brownlee a pen.

"I'm dreadfully sorry," she said biting her lip, "I think there's been some terrible mistake. We didn't order any food from you so I'm afraid you'll have to take this back."

"There's been no mistake, madam," explained the man, scanning his clipboard. "It says here that a Mr Muse called our store yesterday to say he'd forgotten to cancel his Christmas food order with us but he wished for the guests in his house to take delivery of it in his place. Are you Mrs Brownlee?"

"Yes," she whispered in disbelief.

"I believe Mr Muse has left a message for you." He turned to the next sheet on his clipboard. "Ah yes, here it is. It says, 'I don't want this food to go to waste so please would you do me the honour of accepting it with my very best Christmas wishes. Enjoy the feast' There, isn't that nice?"

"Nice? called Mr Brownlee from the top of the stairs, "It's a flippin' miracle!"

Mrs Brownlee closed the door and stared in wonder at the beautiful blue and gold boxes that were almost too gorgeous to open. She'd never been able to afford anything from that shop before, let alone have six huge boxes full of its produce.

"You see?" said her husband as he padded down the stairs to take a closer look. "It's a sign. Everything is going to be OK. I really think this is the start of something big. New changes, new opportunities. Life is going to be great, guys, you wait and see." A sharp pang of guilt hit Bertie square in the guts. She had failed him terribly and he had absolutely no idea. How on earth was she going to put this right?

To take her mind off things, she helped her mum unpack all of the food. It took them more than an hour, largely because they cooed over everything they unearthed. There was a huge turkey and every conceivable vegetable, sauce and condiment to accompany it. Then there was an assortment of the finest puddings, desserts, chocolates, sweets, crisps, snacks, drinks and liqueurs, even some Christmas crackers with luxury prizes inside. It was all of the finest quality money could buy. She still couldn't help but worry about her dad's jobless situation but she took comfort in the fact that they would have enough food to last them for at least a month.

Meanwhile, a long soak in the bath and a short nap had helped Mr Brownlee to feel human again. Later on, while his wife was out delivering the paintings to the village hall for the auction, he, Bertie and Billy set about the tradition of badly decorating Mum's Christmas cake.

Bertie had mixed up some icing sugar and butter in a bowl ready to spread over the cake to create a snow scene but, when she wasn't looking, her dad sneaked a drop of red food colour in and it turned the icing a pretty shade of pink. Bertie giggled as she spread the pink snow icing over the cake and the boys went to find some festive figures to put on the top.

It was then that they discovered Mrs Brownlee had forgotten to bring the cake decorations. It was always Billy's job to put the people on top so he was understandably upset.

"Not to worry, Billy," said Dad. "I'm sure Mr Muse will have something in these cupboards that we can use." He began rummaging around in the kitchen in search of replacements.

"Bingo!" he cried, pulling a box marked 'Cake Decorations' from a top shelf.

They took everything out of the box and found some cake ribbon, candles and numerous little figures to top a cake. They didn't have much to work with but all the same, they were immensely proud of themselves.

When Mum returned, she was presented with a pink Christmas cake trimmed with a "Happy Birthday" ribbon around the edge. It was topped with a little golfer, a skiing polar bear, a bride and groom, a plastic number 40 and a candle in the shape of a champagne bottle.

"Oh my goodness, it's beautiful!" she declared. "I think this is your best yet guys. Who needs Santa when you've got a handsome golfer?"

In that moment, Bertie felt safe and warm within the comfortable craziness of her family and, for a moment, it felt like every other Christmas Eve at the Brownlee's. But it wasn't. It was very different. Too different. Horribly different. Just for a moment she didn't want to think about how she'd messed things up for her whole family, she didn't even want to admit that deep down she wished she'd never found this fancy house and discovered Dream World. She just wanted to pretend that none of it had ever happened and that everything was normal.

CHAPTER 26

At 2pm the family attended the Crib Service at the nearby church, (purely due to Bertie's insistence). An hour later, Polly and TJ came round to the house and the two families waded through the snow up to the village hall for the Christmas Fair. But someone was missing.

"Is your husband not joining us?" Mrs Brownlee asked. She'd found it odd that she still hadn't been told his name. Polly just referred to him as 'Hubby'.

"He's finishing off at work so hopefully he'll join us in a little while. Or at least, that's what he told me. This really isn't his thing at all and I know he's trying to swerve it to be honest but I've insisted he comes to see my painting go up for auction as I'm so proud of it. I never thought I'd be able to create something so beautiful. Thank you again, Bea, for being such a fantastic art teacher."

Mrs Brownlee beamed. "I'm so glad you enjoyed painting, Polly. You've got a natural talent."

"All enhanced by a good bottle of wine no doubt," quipped Mr Brownlee.

When they arrived at the Fair, they found a table and sat down with cups of tea and home made cake. There was quite an impressive turn out despite the weather and the buzz of festive unity amongst the locals warmed Bertie's heart. This was what Christmas was all about. She sat next to TJ and leaned in to whisper so as not to be overheard.

"Are we still on for the song later?"

TJ shrugged. "I don't reckon Dad will turn up. Like Mum said, he hates things like this. He said this morning that it's his idea of hell."

Bertie felt utterly deflated. They'd been so fired up about performing the song and it would be a real body blow if TJ's dad didn't get to hear it.

"Well, we only need him to turn up for the party later and no one can resist a good knees up. Besides, he can't be working that late, it's Christmas Eve."

"You don't know my dad," he said forlornly. "I mean, look at *your* dad, he gets involved with everything and he chats to anyone. Mine can't even be bothered to show up. You're so lucky."

Bertie sighed and told TJ all about the morning's events. "You see nobody's life is perfect. We may be happy but Dad hasn't got a job anymore and who knows what will happen when the money and the food run out."

"He doesn't look worried though does he?" TJ nodded towards Mr Brownlee who was laughing merrily with some local dads.

"No, he isn't worried at all," said Bertie. She wanted to add 'and that's the problem,' but her adventures in Dream World were not for sharing.

Their conversation was halted by the start of the auction. The two mums sat nervously awaiting the turn of their paintings. People were bidding way over the reserve price for sets of luggage, bespoke jewellery and pieces of pottery donated by local businesses and it was clear that this area had some rather wealthy inhabitants.

Soon it was the turn of Polly's painting. The two women had kept the subject of their artwork a secret up until now and the auctioneer pulled off the cover sheet to reveal a picture of an elegant ballerina holding an arabesque pose and carrying a tiny bouquet of delicate flowers. Polly had used subtle shades of brown and beige and it was quite understated yet rather striking. Very impressive for an amateur.

The bidding began and the auctioneer informed the audience that he had a private phone bidder. "I bet that's Hubby," Polly hissed in Mrs Brownlee's ear. "He didn't want to come so he's trying to show his support in another way. You wait until I get my hands on him!"

"Going, once...going twice..." said the auctioneer and with a bang of his hammer, "gone for £500 to the very generous bidder on the telephone."

Polly was not impressed. "Typical!" she spat. "He hasn't even seen it! For all he knows he could've bought a painting of clown on a rollercoaster."

Mrs Brownlee giggled behind her hands. "Your husband might be rubbish but just be thankful he's got a job. I told my husband's boss where to stick his job this morning." Polly gulped loudly and the two women ducked their heads together and gossiped until they were interrupted by the auctioneer's commanding voice.

"Lot number 6, a stunning painting by local artist, Bea Brownlee."

The cover was pulled away from the painting to reveal an incredible work of art that drew gasps of astonishment followed by a reverent silence from the people in the room. She had painted a bare chested man with dark wavy hair, ocean blue eyes and white outstretched wings protruding from his back. He appeared serene and spiritual, inducing a feeling of inner calm to the beholder. The crowd began muttering.

"It's the Angel Gabriel," said one.

"What a divine heavenly body," mused another.

But Bertie knew exactly who it was.

"Mum," she said tugging at her sleeve. "It's breathtaking. What made you paint that?"

"I got the idea from a picture in our bedroom at the house. Actually it's not the Angel Gabriel at all. I forget the name. Errr…it's something beginning with 'M' I think."

"Morpheus?" asked Bertie, knowing full well it was.

"That's it! Morpheus. Well done, brain box. How do you know who that is?"

Bertie had to think quickly. Why would she know who Morpheus was? "We err…we studied Greek Gods in history at school. He's the Son of Sleep."

"Ha! That's a joke," laughed Mum sarcastically. "I've hardly had *any* sleep this week with your father having all these weird dreams. He's woken me up so many times." Bertie thought it best not to mention that Morpheus was also the God of Dreams as that wasn't likely to make her mum feel any better.

The Auctioneer was clearly excited by this lot. "Let's start the bidding at £100. Who would like to bid me £100? Yes, the gentleman over there, thank you, sir. £150? Yes, thank you, madam, £200?" And so the bidding continued. In fact, it went on and on with so many people wanting the painting. The money just kept on rising.

"£1,000 I have over here, any advances on £1,000? Thank you, sir, £1,100. £1,200 with the lady in the hat. £1,300 with the lady standing at the back. £1,400 back to the gentleman here."

Mrs Brownlee was completely stunned by the amount of money people were willing to pay for her art. To her it was just something she'd painted for a bit of fun and mostly under the influence of wine. Nothing special.

The bidding finally narrowed down to just two people, a man in a Christmas jumper and a wealthy looking lady in her late 60s with grey hair and matching grey coat. The room was tense with anticipation as the bidding ping ponged between the two.

"£3,500, sir?" The man thought for moment then nodded. "Ok, £3,600, madam?" the woman agreed without hesitation. "£3,700, sir? Can I tempt you?" The man in the Christmas jumper finally caved in and shook his head. "£3,600 for the first time, £3,600 for the last time, going…going…" the hammer slammed down on the table, "Gone to the lady in the grey coat. Congratulations, madam."

The room erupted in cheers and whoops and Bea was invited to stand up by the applauding crowd. They were curious to know the identity of this incredible artist.

Mr Brownlee kissed and hugged his wife. "Now everyone knows what a talented woman I married."

"I'm so proud of you, Mum," said Bertie.

"Me too!" cried Billy, even though he had no idea what was going on. His dad lifted him up for a Brownlee group hug.

Polly and TJ watched the display of family affection. Here before them was a family with no money, facing a very insecure future, yet despite this they shared so much love and happiness. She put her arm around her son and squeezed him tightly, kissing the top of his head. She had tried so hard to provide him with a happy life and it saddened her deeply that her husband couldn't make the effort to be with them on Christmas Eve.

When the auction was over, everyone stood around the Christmas tree and sang a few carols to get them in the festive mood. Then they all helped move the tables and chairs to make way for the party. The band had started to set up and Mr Brownlee took TJ and Bertie over to ask if they could hijack their set later to perform their song.

Meanwhile, the grey haired lady in the grey coat came over to introduce herself to Mrs Brownlee.

"Hello, Dear, I just wanted to say what a splendid piece that is, I'm absolutely thrilled with it." Despite her frosty appearance, the lady was delightfully warm and friendly with a smile that lit her heavily made-up face. She took Mrs Brownlee's hand and shook it softly. "I'm Elizabeth Smedley, I live at Smedley Hall, just up the hill on the way to Putney."

Mrs Brownlee had seen Smedley Hall when they'd walked Barry the other day. It was a huge stone building, very regal with lead lattice windows and a turreted roof, set back from the road in acres of land. She concluded that Mrs Smedley must be the lady of the manor and she wondered for a moment if perhaps she should curtsey.

"It's a pleasure to meet you, Mrs Smedley. I'm so pleased that my painting raised so much money for the charity, thank you."

"Please, call me Elizabeth," she insisted, "and the pleasure is all mine. It's not every day that I get to meet someone with such a rare talent. Tell me, do you have any of your work in a gallery?"

The two women chatted for some time while the others continued to help prepare the hall. As luck would have it, the band was made up of a group of dads from Barnes and they were more than happy to let two youngsters (and a not so young Brian Brownlee) join them in entertaining everyone that evening.

After a short while, the lights dimmed and some music started playing. Not one for parties, Mrs Smedley said her goodbyes to Mrs Brownlee and handed her a card before being escorted off by her chauffeur. After she'd gone, Mrs Brownlee came over to rejoin her friends and family with a strangely bewildered expression.

"You were talking for a long time, what was that all about?" her husband asked.

Polly was concerned. "Are you OK, Bea? You look a bit pale."

Bertie moved a lock of hair away from her Mum's face. "Yeah, Mum, you do look pale. What's the matter?"

One by one Mrs Brownlee looked everyone in the eye. "You're not going to believe this," she whispered.

"What?" asked her husband impatiently. Everyone moved in closer to hear over the music.

"That was Mrs Smedley, from Smedley Hall – you know that big place up the road?" Her audience nodded keenly. "It turns out that she loved my work so much, she wants to commission two more paintings and she's going to give me £3,000 for each one. And that's just for starters, she wants me to paint many more after that with a view to exhibiting my work in a gallery!"

Everyone stood in open-mouthed silence for a moment before jumping up and down, cheering in jubilation. When the euphoria of the moment had died down Bertie's thoughts turned to her dad's dream with the muddy lake and the tiger and how her mum had pulled her dad to safety. It all began to make sense now. So did this mean it would be her mum who would bring in the money from now on? If so, would Dad be a stay-at-home parent? Maybe *that* was his new path - to be with his children. She hadn't thought of that! After all the big adventures she'd had in Dream World, she had imagined far grander things for her dad than child minding his own children and she couldn't help feeling more than a little disappointed. It seemed such an anticlimax to such an exciting adventure but if this was going to make him happy then that was fine by her. Perhaps he had got off that train in his dream after all.

CHAPTER 27

A festive darkness had descended on Barnes and the snow continued to fall, silently filling in footprints and re-covering shovelled driveways.

The party in the village hall was in full swing and the DJ was doing a fantastic job of bringing generations of families together to throw wild and crazy shapes on the dance floor. The band was preparing to play their first song and TJ and Bertie kept watch on the door.

"Dad's still not here." TJ was beginning to give up all hope of his father turning up at all. Bertie really couldn't bear to see her friend so downhearted but she'd almost run out of ways to keep his spirits lifted. She was starting to think TJ's sad didn't deserve all the effort they'd gone to, to please him.

"There's still an hour and a half left," she said with as much optimism as she could muster. "The band are on in a minute and do you know what? Even if he doesn't show up, we'll do the song anyway. For us, yeah?"

TJ gave her a weak smile. "I'm going to get a drink, want one?" She shook her head and watched him trudge over to the bar with his head bowed. Polly took TJ's seat.

"Is he OK?" she asked.

Bertie shook her head. "Not really. He'd be fine if his dad was here though."

Polly heaved a heavy sigh. "Oh Bertie, I know. I can't tell you how fed up I am about it but his father is a law unto himself. I'm at the end of my tether but I don't want to rock the boat, it's Christmas. I can't risk causing an argument and upsetting TJ."

Bertie stared at Polly in disbelief. "But don't you see? He's already upset. I doubt he could be *more* upset." She could feel herself getting het up. "Do you know, TJ has written a song for his dad and he wanted us to perform it for him tonight. We had it all planned. He wanted to show his dad how much he loves him and above all, he desperately wanted his approval. So you see, Polly, nothing can upset him more than his dad not wanting to spend Christmas Eve with him. I watched my mum take a risk this morning by losing my dad his job and that risk has paid off, so if there was ever a time to take a chance, this is it." She knew she'd overstepped the mark but she really didn't care – it needed to be said. Luckily, Polly took it surprisingly well.

"You're right, Bertie. You're absolutely right," she said as if seeing the light for the first time. "I'm going to sort this out once and for all. Thank you. Thank you for making me see sense." With that, she jumped up, pulled her phone from her pocket and disappeared off.

A short while later, the band launched into their first song with an explosion of sound and the residents of Barnes showed their appreciation by cheering, dancing and singing along. The Brownlee's loved any opportunity to let their hair down and were taking up more than their fair share of space on the dance floor. Bertie had dragged TJ up to dance but he was just doing what she called the shoe gazing shuffle.

"Oi! Dude," she mocked. "You're not in LA now, you're in a village hall with a load of very normal people. And don't let your dad ruin your fun. Come on, forget about everything and enjoy yourself for once." She held his gaze and proceeded to do a comedy dance involving lots of hip twisting and strange hand flicking. He looked up at her from under his fringe and after a brief moment of apprehension, dropped his super cool façade and busted some great moves, causing quite a stir among the young female population of the village.

Polly had reappeared and she and Mrs Brownlee were having the time of their lives down at the front showing the youngsters how it's really done.

"I don't think I've ever seen my mum so relaxed. She's loving this!" TJ shouted across to Bertie.

"She's been hanging around with my mum for too long, she has that affect on people I'm afraid."

"I love it!" he laughed. "She's like a different person. She's so chilled out and happy." They watched their mum's waving their arms in the air and shaking their booty to the music. They looked like a pair of giggly teenagers who'd grown up together.

The band played hit after hit from a whole set of old and new chart songs but just when they had everyone out of their seats, disaster struck. The power cut off, bringing the music to a crashing end and plunging the village hall into complete darkness.

"Nooooo!" jeered the villagers in unison, clearly distraught by their fun ending before it had truly begun.

"It's a power cut. Look, the street lights are out. Must be the weather," said a man peering out of the window.

"How am I going to cook my turkey now?" came a woman's voice from the darkness. Laughter broke out, lightening the mood in the hall. For a moment or two there was a lot of murmuring before one voice, clear and authoritative, spoke out over the crowd. It was Polly.

"Right, who wants to continue the party?" she yelled. Her question was met with a resounding, 'Yeah!'

"OK," she hollered, regaining their attention. "The pub will still be open. They've got a piano and, Brian, you can play us some songs that we can sing along to, right?"

Mr Brownlee raised his hand. "I'm up for that."

Everyone cheered excitedly in agreement with Polly's plan and they all piled out of the village hall and snaked their way around the corner to the pub by the pond.

The pub landlord didn't know what had hit him when half of the village piled in but he welcomed everyone with open arms (and an open till) as they all rushed in singing Christmas songs and making themselves at home.

The owner of the minimarket on the high street popped back to her shop and returned to the pub minutes later with packets of tea lights. Everyone helped light the little candles and dotted them around the bar and the tables, creating a romantic, magical glow.

Meanwhile, Bertie, TJ and Mr Brownlee quickly nipped back to the house and grabbed two acoustic guitars, tambourines and as many percussion instruments as they could carry back with them.

Once back at the pub, Brian Brownlee sat down at the piano and began tinkling the ivory keys to get the crowd warmed up. He played some classic Christmas songs mixed in with some Beatles numbers that he thought the majority of people would know the words to. The dads from the band played the percussion instruments and they drummed on the tables to accompany Mr Brownlee on the piano. The atmosphere was building and everyone was in sky-high spirits, waving drinks in the air and singing along at the tops of their voices.

Bertie was so impressed by the way Polly had taken control of the situation and she wanted to thank her for rescuing the night from complete disaster. But when she scanned the room to find her, she was nowhere to be seen. By chance, she glanced out of the window to see if it was still snowing and spotted Polly talking very animatedly on her mobile. She seemed angry, like she was really having a go at someone and Bertie hoped with all her heart that it was that stubborn husband of hers. In fact, she had a good mind to take the phone from Polly and tell him what she thought of him too.

"Bertie, Bea, Billy, come and sing with me," called Mr Brownlee. "Ladies and gentlemen, this is a song that I wrote about little children on Christmas Eve. It's called,

'Santa's Wish'. Once you know the words, please feel free to join in."

Bertie apprehensively joined her family at the piano. She hadn't sung in public since her school friends had made fun of her and she didn't want to run the risk of it happening all over again. Noting her anxiety, her dad reached for her hand and pulled her closer.

"No one knows us here, Hen," he shouted in her ear. "We can make idiots of ourselves and it doesn't matter. Who cares?" She scanned the rowdy crowd surrounding her and he was right, she didn't recognise one face other than her family and two friends. She smiled openly at her dad who grinned back at her and they launched into the silly song, much to the delight of the crowd. The simple chorus didn't take the people long to learn and soon the Brownlee's had the whole pub singing along and chanting, 'Santa won't come if you don't go to bed'. The applause at the end of the song was deafening and Bertie couldn't stop beaming with pride. She no longer cared what those nasty schoolgirls thought of her, she loved performing and she would never let anyone or anything stop her again.

"Thank you, everyone, thank you so much. Would you like to hear another song?" Mr Brownlee asked his attentive audience. Once again they cheered and clapped in response.

Just then the pub door slowly opened and Bertie watched Polly reappear. She was followed by a mysterious man who slid in through the doors behind her and propped himself up against the wall in the half-light. He was wearing a fedora hat pulled down over his face and he stood with his arms folded, trying too hard to go unnoticed. Bertie's eyes darted over at TJ who smiled and waved at the man. He made his way over to Bertie, mouthing the words, "My dad's here!" She felt a slight rumble of excitement in her stomach. She couldn't believe the elusive dad had finally made an appearance, even if it was an obviously reluctant one. She gave TJ the thumbs up while her dad introduced the next song.

"OK, erm…this is one I wrote some time ago and it sounds much better when my daughter, Bertie sings it. "It's called 'Finding My Way Back Home.' Band, join in with the percussion when you want."

It was TJ's turn to give Bertie the thumbs up and he joined the audience in a now captive silence as the talents of his friend wowed the crowd. Her voice was so pure and clear and she hit every note with such conviction and accuracy. When it came to the chorus she had everyone clapping along to the bouncy rhythm and when they sang along, she sang the harmony.

> 'Cos with you I know I'm not going it alone
> And I'm finding my way back home.
> Back home
> Back home
> Yeah, I'm finding my way back home'.

Chants of "more" and "encore" filled the pub when the song ended and a woman's voice shouted, "You're a little star!" The crowd cheered in agreement and Bertie felt her cheeks flush with a mixture of embarrassment and pride. When the noise died down, she cleared her throat and spoke.

"Thank you so much, everyone. Erm…there is somebody here who really *is* a star. A superstar in fact and he's written a song about someone who means the world to him. We'd very much like to perform it for you, if you don't mind?"

The crowd cheered once again and Bertie picked up an acoustic guitar. She handed it to her friend and they both looked over at his dad who was still hiding in the shadows.

"Ok, everyone, this is TJ."

There was a ripple of applause as he nervously took the guitar and slung the strap over his head. He took one more look at his dad who had taken a step forward and was staring straight at him. He didn't look happy. TJ gave a dry swallow and hung his head. He had so much to lose by doing this and he would have run out of the pub there and then if he hadn't glanced over at Bertie. She winked at him and gave him another little thumbs up.

"For us, yeah?" she said. His frightened face softened and his tense shoulders lowered a little.

"For us," he said.

A hush fell across the crowd as they waited for the two youngsters to perform. TJ took a deep breath and placed his fingers on the guitar strings. In an instant the room was filled with the thrilling sound of expert strumming as he thrashed out catchy chords that made everyone suddenly cheer and leap to their feet. He had them all dancing and clapping and whooping with enjoyment and he'd only just started. The piano dropped into the mix and the dads on percussion picked up the rhythm and the bass. By the time Bertie hit the chorus, the crowd was whipped up into a thronging mass of euphoria, and she had them punching the air and pogoing around the room as she sang.

When the song drew to an end, TJ hit them with a strumming frenzy only ever heard by the most accomplished of players and the crowd gradually stopped leaping around to watch this child genius at work. He took the tempo from the upbeat stomp, progressively down until he was gently picking at the strings and playing an enchanting melody. Bertie joined in with soft, wispy vocals to sing the chorus once more, only this time expressing the words as if speaking straight to the man for whom they were intended:

You're my inspiration
When you entertain a nation
You're my soul
You're my energy
 My light

Yeah cos you're the man that made me
But your time is what escapes me
Only you
Can change the wrong to right.
Oh yeah you, should be living in the light

When she had uttered the last word of the song, the whole room exploded in a roar of applause, cheers, whistles and foot stamping approval. Bertie and TJ stood to take their bows and were swamped with people bombarding them with questions and compliments. For a moment, Bertie thought she was having one of her daydreams. But no, this time it was for real and it felt epic.

Moments later, TJ grabbed Bertie's hand and pulled her away from the throng of people. As they passed Mr Brownlee, TJ tapped him on the arm.

"Can you two come with me to see my dad? I don't want to face him on my own." More than happy to oblige, they eagerly followed TJ towards Polly and the mysterious man in the hat.

"Oh, and Mr Brownlee," TJ said stopping halfway, "brace yourself, OK?"

"Brace myself? Why?" asked Mr Brownlee nervously as he continued to chase TJ through the mass of people. "Your dad isn't going to hit me is he? I only helped you write a song, it's not like I taught you to play the guitar or anything."

They came to a stop in the far corner of the pub and TJ sheepishly approached his dad. But before his dad could speak, TJ thrust his friends forward.

"Dad, this is my new friend Bertie and this is her dad, Mr Brownlee."

Mr Brownlee stepped forward, offering to shake TJ's dad by the hand.

"I'm Brian," he said confidently. "It's nice to finally meet you. Sorry I don't know your name." He looked up at the man who still had most of his face hidden by his hat.

TJ's dad slowly lifted the brim of his fedora to reveal a face Brian Brownlee knew very well. Very well indeed.

"Hi," said the man in a husky voice. "It's nice to meet you too. I'm Tiger. Tiger Jonz."

CHAPTER 28

Most people dream of meeting their idols. They imagine all of the witty and intelligent things they would say to impress and amuse them. Unfortunately this wasn't the case for Mr Brownlee. The poor man was frozen to the spot with his mouth hanging open and his eyes wide like a startled owl. He was so dumbstruck by the pop god of all pop gods who stood before him that Bertie felt compelled to shove her embarrassing dad sharply to one side.

She was sure *she* knew how to behave in front of her idol – she'd daydreamed about it enough times. But, as her father had painfully discovered, real life wasn't quite so easy. She felt her mouth dry up and her heart beat faster. She glared up at Tiger Jonz, *the* Tiger Jonz with his uber cool clothes, floppy fringe and trademark nose ring and, she too, was lost for words. What do you say to the man whose music was the soundtrack to your childhood? Then she had a reality check. He wasn't just a superstar, he was a dad who had been neglecting his son - her friend.

"Hi, Mr Jonz," she said boldly. "I'm glad you could make it at last."

"So am I, Miss," Tiger replied with a slight smile. "That's quite a voice you've got there for someone so young. I'm impressed."

He smiled down at her and she was quite taken aback by how softly spoken and timid he appeared. She would have expected someone of his celebrity status to be loud and overconfident but he was quite the opposite. For a moment she'd allowed herself to be flattered by his compliment but then she caught sight of the dejected expression on TJ's face.

"Did you like the song? TJ wrote it. Went down a storm with everyone didn't it?"

Tiger shifted from one foot to another and exhaled through pursed lips. TJ and Bertie shot each other a glance and awaited his response with fear and trepidation.

"When did you learn to play the guitar, Son?" His voice had turned cold and stern. TJ hung his head. He didn't reply. Sensing the tension, Bertie interjected.

"He's an incredible guitarist, don't you think? Dad calls him a child genius, don't you, Dad?" She nudged Mr Brownlee who was still awestruck by his idol.

"Oh! Gosh, y…yeah…phenomenal," he stammered. "Far better than me." But Tiger didn't even register the bumbling buffoon of a man at his side.

"You went behind my back, Son. I thought we'd talked about this; you're a bright kid with a bright future. You should be concentrating on your studies not messing around with music."

TJ didn't utter a word. Instead he stood staring at his feet, his body tense and awkward as he fought hard to stop the tears that threatened to fill his eyes. He made an attempt to say something in his defence but was so overcome with emotion that his voice cracked and he ran off before any tears fell.

"Dad, go after him," Bertie ordered. Mr Brownlee finally broke his fixed gaze from his idol and did as he was told.

Bertie looked at Tiger and he looked nervously back at her.

"Right!" she said firmly. "I don't care who you are or how much I love your music, you are behaving like an idiot."

Tiger's eyebrows shot up his forehead and his mouth fell open. No one ever raised their voice at him, especially not an eleven year old girl.

"I'm sorry, Bertie is it?" he asked calmly.

"Yes, Bertie Brownlee," she confirmed, trying desperately to behave and sound older than her years.

"Bertie," he repeated. "Listen, I know this seems harsh to you but I love my son to bits and I really only have his best interests at heart. I don't want him wasting his life on music."

"What, like you have you mean?" she asked with smug sarcasm. "Yeah, it didn't work out too well for you did it, all those million selling albums and worldwide tours."

Tiger couldn't stop a smile forming on his lips. Whoever this kid was, she was good.

"You don't understand," he said, sympathetically. "I don't want him following me into the music business because I want him to be a normal kid with a normal life. That's all. I love him so much I just want to protect him."

"But, Mr Jonz, seriously? Do you not realise? Music *is* his normal. Music is his life, just as it is yours. If your dad had told you not to play the guitar when you were young, you'd have probably left home, right?" She raised her eyebrows at him and he chuckled at her.

"Yeah, you're right, I probably would have." He shook his head in disbelief and wondered if this girl whom he'd only just met was some kind of freakishly young psychotherapist.

Bertie knew she was being out of line but she felt responsible for causing a rift between TJ and his mega famous dad. She really wanted to let rip at Tiger and make him see sense but he was being so annoyingly nice, plus he seemed quite nervous which almost made her feel sorry for him. She took a deep breath to calm herself, then selected a less aggressive tone.

"The fact that TJ has taught himself to play the guitar to such an absurdly good level at such a young age just shows that he's got a natural talent - a gift. And he's a natural songwriter too. I'm afraid it's my fault that he performed tonight. I wanted you to see how fantastic he is because I thought if you heard him play you'd be proud of him. I encouraged him to write that song and I even got my dad to help him. So if you want to be angry at anyone, be angry with me."

Tiger smiled sweetly, a smile she'd seen a million times on TV and in magazines.

"OK, kid, I get it. You're TJ's friend and you're trying to help him. I wish I'd had friends like you when I was his age. But you're too young to understand. You've got a normal life and you have no idea what it's like living in the spotlight. It's not all it's cracked up to be, you're life isn't your own. Imagine having the world watching your every move and having an opinion on everything that you do. I just want to protect my son from all of that as much as I possibly can."

"No, you're right I don't know what that's like," she agreed with a sigh, "but if you want a normal life for TJ then you have to do normal things like spending quality time with him. You have to live in one place for longer than a few weeks to give him the chance to make good friends and settle into a proper school like other kids of his age. You have to get involved with his interests and hobbies and you have to do normal things that normal people do, even if it means going to a village fair because it will make him happy. Yes you're famous but so what? This is London; no one takes any notice. People will get over the whole fame thing once they get to know you and once you stop hiding in the shadows."

Tiger's arms were clenched tightly across his body and his head was bowed. He said nothing. Bertie saw such pain and sadness in his face. He looked like a lost little boy, the complete opposite to the exuberant pop star that she'd always seen bounding across stadium stages.

She glanced behind her to see that her dad had reclaimed his seat at the piano and people were gathering around him. She looked back at Tiger and reached out to give his arm a gentle squeeze.

"Come on," she said warmly. "Come and join in the fun. Lighten up. Let your hair down. It's Christmas!" She gave him a big smile and then proceeded to drag the

215

reluctant superstar away from the safety of the dimly lit corner and over to his wife and son who were sat with her mum and Billy next to the piano.

"OK!" boomed Mr Brownlee, "It's time for a bit of audience participation. Everyone copy me." He stamped his foot on the ground three times then clapped. The crowd in the pub put down their drinks and joined in.

"And again," he instructed.

Stomp, stomp, stomp clap

Stomp, stomp, stomp clap

"Then seven stomps and a clap." The audience obliged;

Stomp, stomp, stomp, stomp, stomp, stomp, stomp clap

"Great! Now I'm going to sing a song that I wrote just after my son was born. When I get to the chorus I want you to join in with the three stomps and the clap. You can sing along too - it's so simple, it goes like this:"

You and me (clap)

She makes three (clap)

He, she, you, me, family (clap)

He played the piano and the audience sang, clapped and stomped enthusiastically along to the repetitive chorus.

"Fantastic!" cried Mr Brownlee, "great stuff. Right, TJ, can you grab that guitar and just join in when you get a feel for the song."

TJ shook his head and dropped his gaze to the floor. Mr Brownlee pretended not to notice and continued to get the crowd going.

"If anyone wants to play the other guitar they can, or grab the percussion instruments. In fact just bang, tap or hit anything you can find to create a rhythm. Let's go!"

His fingers danced over the piano keys as he bashed out the infectiously catchy song and the crowd became one united band as they joined in with gusto, bashing tambourines, slapping table tops and tapping glasses and stomping and chanting the chorus.

Tiger looked around at all of the people having the time of their lives with total carefree abandon. Even his wife was dancing and singing at the top of her voice, laughing loudly with her new friend. He hadn't seen her this happy in a long time. The only person in the whole place not joining in, apart from himself, was his son. He was sat on a stool with his head bowed. Tiger's heart lurched. TJ looked broken - a child rejected by his father. What had he done to his own son? How could he have been so selfish as to stop him from doing something he loved? Bertie's words resonated in his head. He hesitated for a moment then leapt to his feet and grabbed one of the acoustic guitars. Then he grabbed the other one and held it out to his son. Over the sound of the music and merriment TJ just about made out the words that he'd waited all of his life to hear.

"Play the guitar with me, Son."

TJ lifted his eyes towards his dad and was taken aback to see that he was smiling down at him.

"Please take it," urged Tiger as he thrust the guitar into TJ's hand. "I want to see if you're as good as your old man."

TJ gingerly took the guitar from his dad and placed the strap over his head. His dad did the same and they stood face-to-face, guitars in hand. The minute they strummed together, they felt a connection they'd never felt before. A sudden bolt of energy surged through them, bonding the two estranged spirits and fusing the connection that had been lost for so many years. The one thing that Tiger had tried so hard to keep from his son was the one thing that united them. Music had been their missing link and now music was their healing.

The energy in the pub was explosive as each and every person performed together, strumming, stomping, clapping, banging, shaking and singing at the tops of their voices. Being in the company of rock royalty may have had a little something to do with the atmosphere shifting up a gear and Mr Brownlee totally milked this as he kicked back his piano stool and danced about theatrically whilst hammering the piano keys. Not to be out done, Polly, Mrs Brownlee, Bertie and Billy all climbed on top of the tables and danced wildly while TJ and Tiger started leaping about, windmilling their arms as they struck the strings of their guitars. The crowd pogoed up and down with their arms around each other's shoulders and the whole pub rocked out to the insanely infectious song. On and on it went, verse after chorus after verse until eventually, Mr Brownlee brought the number to a dramatic climax with a wall of sound from everyone giving it all they had before they collapsed in a weary heap of exhilaration and exhaustion.

Bertie looked around for TJ and her eyes pricked with tears of joy as she saw Tiger give his son a high five followed by a lasting hug. They looked like long lost family members, reunited after years apart. But then again, they kind of were.

CHAPTER 29

Much like the end of a concert, the party in the pub disbanded and the revellers said their goodbyes and made their way home. As they were leaving, the streetlights flickered and flashed back to life as the power in the village was restored. In the distance a lady's voice could be heard shouting, "Thank God for that, I can cook my turkey now!"

The Brownlee and Jonz families trudged together through the snow towards their respective houses, still buzzing from the events of the evening. Tiger and TJ linked arms and chatted while Bertie and the women hung back to observe them.

"Look," said Polly, gesturing towards her husband and son. "It's been a very long time since I saw the two of them so close. It really is quite wonderful."

"It almost went horribly wrong though didn't it?" sighed Bertie. "I'm so relieved it turned out the way it did."

"And I'm so glad you gave me a stern talking to, Bertie. If you hadn't, I doubt I would've taken action. I needed that push from you." She put her arm around Bertie and gave her a squeeze.

Concerned that her mum would discover how rude she'd been to grown–ups, Bertie rapidly changed the subject. "Well at least we all know what 'TJ' stands for now then. Is it Tiger Jonz or Tiger Junior?"

"Tiger Junior," Polly confirmed, "I suppose we should call him TJJ!"

"More importantly we now know what Hubby's real name is," laughed Mrs Brownlee. "He's not quite the computer bore we were expecting."

Polly gave an embarrassed giggle. "Yeah, sorry about all the secrets. TJ has been really let down in the past by people just wanting to be his friend because of who his dad is, especially in LA. So we made the decision some time ago not to mention it to anyone unless we had to. He's absolutely loved spending time with you guys these past few days - he's found it really liberating."

"Well nothing's going to change," said Bertie. "TJ wasn't put off me by my dad and I shan't think any differently of him because of his!"

"What I want to know," said Mrs Brownlee, pensively, "is what you said to your husband to make him come down to the pub? I really didn't think he was going to turn up."

Polly leant in to whisper so that her husband wouldn't hear. "I told him, if he didn't leave the recording studio and get there in five minutes, I would divorce him and take everything he's got. He's never been so scared in his life!" The two of them cackled so loudly they could be heard half way across the green.

Meanwhile, Tiger gave TJ another hug. "I've been a bit of an idiot haven't I, Son?"

"Yep, you have," he said nudging his dad sideways. Tiger laughed and hugged him again.

"I can't tell you how proud I am of you right now. You know, something your friend Bertie said to me really made me realise that I was behaving like my dad. He was always telling me to get a proper job and he never believed in me. That used to hurt so badly and I resented him greatly for it. There I was doing the same thing to you. How dumb can you get?"

"Pretty dumb as it turns out," smirked TJ.

"I'm sorry I've been shutting you out, Son. All the press and the unwelcome attention have made me a nervous wreck over the years and I've just grown too over protective of you, you know? But I realise that's something I've gotta overcome, for your sake. The pressure to write a new album as good as the last one has gotten the better of me too these past months and I've neglected you but that's gonna change as of right now. OK?"

"Thanks, Dad," said TJ smiling broadly. He was so incredibly happy he felt like all of his Christmases had come at once. Then he felt something else – a freezing snowball on the back of his head. "Bertie Brownlee! Your luck has just expired!" he said menacingly as he gathered snow in his hands and prepared his ammunition for a revenge attack.

As the three youngsters snowballed each other, the two dads fell into step.

"You've got a great family, you know that?" said Tiger. "That daughter of yours is one clever little lady. She taught me the biggest lesson of my life tonight. In fact, she taught me a few."

"She's turned out to be quite a feisty one lately. I'm sorry if she's been a bit forthright," said Mr Brownlee, apologetically. He felt ridiculously nervous in Tiger's company but fought so hard not to let it show. "I hear she gave Polly a talking to as well. It's not like her to be so outspoken."

"No, no, she had every right to put me in my place and she sure did that! Polly told me about her conversation with Bertie and do you know what? She needed it too. We both did. If it wasn't for your daughter, I think I would've been spending Christmas on my own. It's funny how it takes a kid to show you the way sometimes isn't it?" Not knowing what else to say Mr Brownlee opted for small talk.

"How *are* you spending Christmas tomorrow? Will you just be here in Barnes or are you visiting family?"

"Nah, just us," sniffed Tiger. "Minus the turkey."

"Oh, are you vegetarian?"

"Oh god no! No I got a call earlier from the restaurant up the hill. They've had to cancel our Christmas dinner tomorrow - something to do with the weather. What with everything going on tonight, I haven't had the chance to break it to Polly that our Christmas dinner will be out of a tin."

"Have you tried booking anywhere else?"

"No point; everywhere will be fully booked. Just when I was making amends with the wife too. She's not going to be happy."

"Come to us," blurted Mr Brownlee before his brain had engaged with his mouth.

"Huh?" said Tiger, throwing him a strange look.

"Come and have dinner at our house. We had a massive food delivery today and we'll never be able to eat it all ourselves. You'd be doing us a favour." Tiger didn't answer straight away. He wasn't used to socialising with people he didn't know, it usually made him anxious. But for some reason, he felt comfortable in this family's presence. Plus he knew it would please his son no end.

"Hey man, that's most generous of you. We'd be honoured. You may have just saved my marriage."

Mr Brownlee had to fight the urge to punch the air and shout "YES!!" Instead he maintained his composure. When he woke up that morning his life was quite normal. Tonight it was quite the opposite and to top it all, a very famous Tiger was coming to tea.

CHAPTER 30

High on the excitement of the evening, Bertie didn't think she'd ever get to sleep that night. Her dad was bordering on hysterical when they'd got in, running laps around the living room screaming, 'Tiger Jonz is coming for Christmas!' over and over again like a child who'd consumed too much sugar. Eventually, the exhaustion of the day's events caught up with her and she fell into a deep and unbroken slumber.

Instead of arriving at her D-zone that night with the Tudor cottage and its eternal festive decorations, she found herself striding up a vibrant red carpet towards a majestic fairy-tale castle with tall spires and pretty waving flags.

It was night time and the pathway to the castle was lit by thousands of tiny tea lights, just like the ones they'd used to illuminate the pub earlier that evening. She remembered Curtis saying something about a party when he had rescued her from the train dream so she assumed this must be the venue. It was all terribly grand and incredibly exciting. She felt like royalty as she trod the red carpet towards the floodlit castle and a host of butterflies fluttered in her stomach as she approached the stone steps, which led to huge wooden arched doors. Without warning the doors swung open and Stella appeared wearing a beautiful ball gown with a sparkling tiara, glass slippers and silky blonde hair.

"Bertie! It's so lovely to see you again!" she cheered, holding out her arms for an embrace.

"Stella! You're looking very Cinderella this evening. I love the shoes." Stella giggled and gave a little twirl to show off the intricate golden embroidery on her pale blue dress.

"I probably should have gone for the Snow White look, seeing as I've got naturally dark hair but I couldn't resist this outfit." She linked arms with Bertie and escorted her through the doors into a large circular hallway with a mesmerizing mosaic tiled floor.

"Mr Muse sent me to greet you. He hadn't had a chance to formally invite you himself, what with the terrible business of the recurring train dream. Are you ok?" She showed a genuine look of concern.

"Oh yes, totally fine," said Bertie, brushing off the whole event. "So much has happened since then I'd almost forgotten all about it. I was so lucky that my dad passed out – poor man."

Stella gave a half smile. "That was fortunate...for you I mean, not for your dad, obviously."

"So what's all this about then?" Bertie asked, taking in her surroundings.

"You've come to Morpheus Hall for Mr Muse's annual Christmas party. It's a chance for all Dream Dwellers to get together and celebrate our achievements over the past year. We really look forward to it, it's always so much fun. Now, the theme tonight is fairy tales, in case you haven't guessed. What would you like to wear?"

Being eleven years old, Bertie had had her fill of princess dresses so she was a little stumped. She tried thinking of her favourite Christmas fairy tales but The Little Match Girl and Babushka really weren't that glamorous and as for The Grinch That Stole Christmas, well, she wasn't about to turn up to a ball covered in green fur.

"I think I'll go for something simple." She closed her eyes and imagined her outfit. When she re-opened them, Stella was looking on admiringly.

"Little Red Riding Hood. Good choice. You're quite fond of a red coat aren't you?"

"You can't go wrong with red. And look, I've been baking for Grandma. How thoughtful of me," she said, swinging a little hand woven basket full of delicious cup cakes.

"We *shall* go to the ball," Stella laughed. She linked her arm through Bertie's and they slinked off down a corridor leading from the circular hallway. At the end, two footmen opened another set of large oak doors and Bertie stepped into the most magnificent ballroom. It was straight out of a fairy tale.

"Woah!" she gasped as her eyes drank in the glorious sight. On the walls hung vast mirrors framed by ornately sculptured gold carvings. Keeping watch from the high painted ceiling were cherubs and heavenly beings and below them hung huge chandeliers like golden clouds of raining diamonds. The floor-to-ceiling windows were draped in heavy velvet of the deepest red, matching the fabric on the thrones that surrounded the room. The opulence and majesty of the hall was surely fit for royalty, not an ordinary little girl like herself.

As they made their way across the room, Bertie looked on in wonder at the costumes of the Dream Dwellers. She found it highly amusing to watch Goldilocks chatting happily to Rapunzel and two ugly sisters sharing drinks with Rumpelstiltskin. A lady dressed as Snow White swept past and gave Bertie a little wave before disappearing off.

"Do you know who she is?" Stella asked. Bertie was embarrassed to admit that she didn't have a clue.

"She was your supply teacher when Mrs Bland took a break. Remember?"

"Ohhh! Yes! Bertie cried. The lovely lady who didn't tell me off for daydreaming. She's a Dream Dweller? No wonder she was so forgiving!"

"Mr Muse sent her. He thought you needed a break. Oh, there he is!" Before Bertie had chance to take it all in, Stella had dragged her off through the crowd of partygoers towards the centre of the hall. "Just look at his costume! It's so *him* don't you think?"

There, holding court in the middle of the room was Mr Muse dressed as Prince Charming.

"Bertie! You're here," he shrilled, causing every head to turn. "I'm so pleased to see you. How are you, my dear girl?"

"I'm great, Mr Muse, thank you for inviting me."

He bear-hugged her too tightly then ushered all three of them over to one side where it was quieter. He took Bertie's hand and squeezed it between both of his.

"I'm so sorry about the train dream, really I am. If your dad hadn't given me those ridiculous high heels to wear I'd have been able to catch you up. I've felt so hideously awful all day."

"Oh gosh, I'm fine, Mr Muse, you mustn't feel bad."

"Oh but I do, I do. I'd promised you everything would be OK and it wasn't."

"Please, forget about it," Bertie insisted. "I may never go on another train for as long as I live but hey, everything worked out well in the end."

"Really? he asked. "Tell me, what's happened?"

Bertie told Mr Muse and Stella all about her mum losing her dad his job, the Christmas Fair with the power cut and how her dad had entertained the whole village with his music and songs.

"He was awesome. You should have seen him," she gushed. "Then - and you won't believe this - his absolute idol Tiger Jonz turned up! Can you believe that?!"

"How come he was there?" Stella asked, disappointingly unimpressed. Bertie explained the whole story about TJ and his relationship with his dad and she noticed a knowing smile forming on Stella's face.

"So, if you hadn't told Polly to take action, and if you hadn't spoken to Tiger the way you did, then he and TJ might never have mended their broken relationship?"

"I guess not."

"Aren't you usually quite a shy sort of girl? Any idea where you found this confidence?" Mr Muse asked, cocking his head to one side like an inquisitive puppy.

Bertie's eyes flicked between her two friends. They were both smiling down at her expectantly.

"Alright, what's going on?" she demanded. "You two are up to something."

They both chuckled. "We *were* up to something but it seems we don't need to be anymore," Stella said, cryptically.

"What? Tell me what you've done!"

Mr Muse placed his hand on Bertie's shoulder the way he usually did when he was about to give one of his long-winded explanations.

"Have you had any dreams lately, Bertie?" he asked.

"Errr…no actually, I haven't. I've been too busy in Dream World with you guys to have time to dream."

"Well, you'd be wrong," he said waggling a pointed finger. "You see it may have appeared to you that you were spending all night in Dream World but time is deceiving here, remember? What seemed like hours to you may only have been a few minutes. The rest of the time I was creating Morpheus dreams for you."

"For me?"

"Uh huh. You," he nodded.

"But why? What did I need help with?"

"Confidence, my dear child, confidence. I thought it was about time you discovered the strength you have within. You no longer need to spend hours hiding away in the background lost in daydreams. You now have the ability to make friends, to speak up for yourself and to make things happen. Plus, you'll no longer let silly girls stop you from doing the things you love . There was no way I was going to let you keep that beautiful voice of yours hidden. When you return to school, I think you'll find you're quite a different person."

She stared into space, contemplating his every word. She *had* changed. He'd helped her to change, and she hadn't even realised.

"But I don't remember any dreams," she insisted.

"You don't need to," came his simple reply. Bertie's strained expression softened and a grin met her lips. She would never have had the confidence to get to know TJ the way she had if it wasn't for Mr Muse's help.

"Thank you," she sighed. "I'm so grateful."

"Well, it was all part of a bigger plan," he said. "You see, Stella's had a lot to do with how things have panned out too, haven't you, Dear."

Stella was beaming. "I have and it's all gone so swimmingly, I'm over the moon!"

Bertie was confused again. "What has?"

"Well, I was working on your mum's dreams," Stella explained. "I could see she needed to reignite her passion for painting and Mr Muse and I knew that it would help with the family finances too."

"Ahh. So that's why I saw you in my dad's dream – you know, when he came out of that water slide. You were there with Mum and Billy."

Stella nodded. "I was showing her she needed to be strong for your dad. Without that he would never have handed his notice in. She certainly sorted his boss out didn't she?!"

"That was funny," Bertie giggled. "Dad and I were so shocked. It was so out of character for my mum."

"Also, there was Polly," said Stella.

"You worked on Polly's dreams as well? This is unbelievable."

"Well, it was about time she found *herself* and stopped hiding in her husband's shadows. I have to say, it wasn't difficult because Polly and your mum hit it off straight away."

"Didn't they just," Bertie remarked. "So you helped them and they helped each other."

"Absolutely. They really inspired one another to make changes for the better."

"But the hardest one to work on was our friend the Tiger," said Mr Muse with a raised eyebrow. Bertie's jaw slowly dropped.

"No way! Don't tell me you were working on Tiger Jonz too. I can't believe it!"

"I have been for quite some time now and I can tell you, he's been a tough nut to crack." Bertie looked at him searchingly, desperate for him to elaborate.

"Tiger has been...shall we say, *stuck* for quite a while due to various different elements of his life not flowing smoothly. He was my main mission. Stella and I have tried so many things to get his life moving again but to no avail. Then I had this brain wave one day. You see I had been doing a little bit of work on you and your family as well and I thought it might help if I merged the two together. Boom! Two for the price of one as they say."

"The way you've made all of this work is pretty clever - you guys are awesome."

Mr Muse threw his head back and laughed openly. "Goodness me I don't know about that, but it has all worked out rather well."

"Amazingly well," Bertie agreed. "Apart from the little matter of a job for Dad. I can't see how being a stay-at-home parent is going to be too fulfilling for him. I really didn't expect that to be his destiny."

"Ahh, yes, well you'll have to wait and see about that won't you," he said giving her a wink and before she could question him further, she was being ushered back into the middle of the hall. "Time to dance, girls. Come on, we need to celebrate our 'awesome' achievements."

Bertie made sure she enjoyed every last remaining minute in this crazy place. She ate too much, drank fizzy drinks, laughed at Mr Muse's dad-dancing and partied until her legs ached and her feet were sore. With their missions accomplished, she knew this might be the last time she would visit Dream World. She didn't dare think about how much she would desperately miss her new friends and the wild adventures they'd taken her on.

After much throwing of shapes on the dance floor, Mr Muse wiped the sweat from his brow and steered the three of them to an open balcony for a moment of quiet and some much needed fresh air.

"That was so much fun," Bertie panted. "It's been quite a night."

"Hasn't it just," said Stella, fanning herself. "Did you see Curtis dressed as Tinkerbell? I didn't think I'd ever stop laughing."

"Oh it's been such a fantastic evening," sighed Mr Muse. "But I'm afraid it has to come to an end for you now, Bertie." His joyful expression fell to one of sorrow and he clasped his hands together, placing his index fingers to his lips as he contemplated his next words.

"I'm not good with goodbyes so let me just say this. You have been a fantastic trainee Dream Dweller. Right from the start you've got stuck in and immersed yourself in the tasks. At times you've shown great initiative and you've taken risks that many experienced Dream Dwellers would avoid at all costs. I mean it when I say that Stella and I really couldn't have completed our tasks without you and you truly deserve the rewards that are due. You're destined for greatness here, Bertie, so I sincerely hope that you'll wish to return when the time is right."

Bertie swallowed hard, trying to force away the lump in her throat. "Thank you so much for everything that you have done for me and my family. You've given us so much. I still have so many questions left unanswered though, like what your first name is and why you dress the way you do. You are the most mysterious man I've ever met but I live in hope that one day, all will be revealed."

"Darling Bertie," he chuckled, "as I always say, all in good time. Maybe when you are next needed here, you'll find the answers you seek. There is so much more to this place than you know. We've merely scratched the surface. Of course, that is if you want to go through all of this again?"

"I do! I definitely do! I'm going to miss you guys so much." Stella noticed the wobble in Bertie's voice so she gave her a big hug. This only made Bertie more emotional and her eyes filled with tears, which set Stella off too.

"Stop it, you two, you'll have me crying next," sniffed Mr Muse who joined in with the hug.

Suddenly, Bertie felt a familiar pulling sensation and she knew it was time to go. She wiped away her tears and blew a kiss.

"Goodbye! And Merry Christmas."

"Until next time my little friend," said Mr Muse with a wave.

And in a moment she was gone.

CHAPTER 31

The snow had continued to fall gently over night, silently refreshing the blank canvas across Barnes.

When Bertie awoke on Christmas morning everything was just how her perfect Christmas should be - dark and snowy outside, cosy and warm inside with just the twinkle of fairy lights for that warming festive glow. The sun made no attempt to come out of hiding all day and not a drop of snow melted. Just perfect.

Mrs Brownlee made everyone open her special presents before doing anything else that morning and judging by the squishy packages, her family knew it would be one of her home made outfits. This year she had excelled herself with onesies for everybody. A snowman for Billy complete with a felt top hat and carrot sticking out of his forehead, a reindeer with the obligatory red nose for Bertie, a rather pretty Elf for herself and a huge round Christmas pudding for Dad. His children roared with laughter at the way his head poked out of the top and his legs looked like skinny twigs in the comedy tartan tights that he'd been made to wear. Outfits on, they ate breakfast then sat around the magnificent Christmas tree in front of the roaring fire to open their huge pile of presents.

"These are just little extra ones from me," said Dad, handing out his gifts. "I bought these a few days ago when I left work early that time." The presents were ripped open in seconds and Bertie was astounded by what was revealed beneath the shiny paper.

"Corr, thanks, Dad," cried Billy. He was holding a furry grisly bear with light up red eyes and a loud roar - just like the one her dad had tamed in his dream.

"These are beautiful!" gasped Mum, as she held up a stunning pair of silver strappy high heels with diamonds across the toes. Bertie stifled the urge to laugh out loud - the last time she'd seen those, they were on Mr Muse's feet in that god forsaken train dream. She had a feeling she knew what hers was going to be before she'd even opened it.

"A pink bunny!" she said, trying to sound surprised. "I love its white fluffy tail."

"Do you know the funny thing?" asked Dad. "I had the strangest dreams about these presents. I can't remember exactly what happened now but I do remember Bertie turning into that pink rabbit."

Billy fell about laughing and Bertie bit her tongue to stop herself from screaming, 'I remember it too and I'm scarred for life!'

Mrs Brownlee had gone all out to serve the most incredible Christmas dinner. It wasn't often she had such top quality food to cook with, which had made the task considerably more enjoyable, and it certainly wasn't every day that they had a world famous pop star coming to dine with them.

When their guests arrived around mid-day, they were met by a Christmas pudding and a reindeer.

"Merry Christmas!" cried Mr Brownlee as he opened the front door. "You'll have to excuse me, I've put on a little Christmas weight." He patted his round pudding like an expectant mum. Polly found him hysterical and even the cool as ice Tiger Jonz cracked a smile behind his pop star shades. Mr Brownlee shepherded them into the house and whispered in Tiger's ear.

"I'll take this off in a minute. I promised the kids I'd wear it until you arrived."

Tiger removed his sunglasses and shook Mr Brownlee's hand.

"Lookin' good, man. Where'd you get that thing?"

"Oh Bea makes us different surprise outfits every year. I always come off worst. Last year I went to the pub dressed as a Christmas bauble. It keeps the kids happy."

"Please, keep it on," said Tiger, dryly. "You've made my day."

The families ploughed their way through the turkey with all the trimmings and by the time they'd finished, the dining room was littered with streamers, pulled crackers and spent party poppers. They retired to the living room where the grown-ups sank into the squishy sofas, groaning and moaning about how they should've stopped at one helping of pudding.

Bertie disappeared for a little while and returned holding a woolly hat and scarf, a pair of her dad's ski gloves, Tiger's sunglasses, a knife and fork, a chopping board and a large bar of chocolate.

"OK," she shouted, to get everyone's attention. "We're going to play a game." She placed everything down on the carpet and sat on the floor. She unwrapped the chocolate and put it on the chopping board. Then she produced a dice from her pocket and began to explain the rules of the game.

"The first person to roll a six has to wear all of these things. Then they must try and cut the chocolate into little squares using the knife and fork until someone else rolls a six. When that happens, *that* person has to wear all of the garments and so it goes on until the chocolate bar is all cut up. The person with the most squares wins."

The grown-ups moaned about having to get up from the squishy sofas and reluctantly plopped themselves on the floor to join the kids. But it wasn't long before their competitive sides kicked in and there was much pantomime booing and jeering each time they rolled anything other than a six.

Polly was the first one to hit the jackpot and got a fit of the giggles when she found it impossible to grip the cutlery with the over-sized gloves. Billy rolled the next six and just managed to get all of the garments on when TJ rolled another. He was really nifty with the knife and fork, despite the hindrance of the outerwear, and stacked up a nice pile of chocolate squares before his dad hit the next six.

"Sorry, Son but your dad's gonna take you down." He snatched the things from TJ and hacked away at the chocolate. He even broke out into a sweat under all the layers of wool, chipping square after square off the huge bar.

"Quick! He can't beat me! Don't let him beat me!" cried TJ and the dice was passed around like a hot rock as everyone tried desperately to roll a six and put a stop to Tiger's winning streak.

"Yeeessss!" screamed Mr Brownlee as the top number landed face up and he whipped the hat off his opponent. Tiger was really miffed and he curled his fingers up to stop Mr Brownlee from getting the gloves off his hands. Mr Brownlee retaliated by stuffing two of Tiger's hard earned chocolate squares into his mouth.

"That's a foul!" protested Tiger and he gave Mr Brownlee a push, sending him rolling backwards in his giant Christmas pudding. Try as he might he couldn't right himself and he was left frantically kicking his little tartan legs in the air like a stranded beetle on it's back.

"Help! I can't get up! Help me!" He was laughing so hysterically that he was too weak to move.

Everyone fell about laughing and Tiger giggled like a five year old as he tried to pull Mr Brownlee to his feet. Unfortunately, their hands slipped and the pudding was sent rolling again, this time settling on his front.

Tiger fell to his knees holding his stomach. "Oh my god, I've never laughed so much in my life. I can't breathe - I think I'm going to die!"

"Me too," came Mr Brownlee's muffled voice. "Please don't let me die in a Christmas pudding."

It took all three of the children and the two women to heave poor Mr Brownlee to his feet while Tiger lay in a helpless heap on the floor. When he was upright once again, Mr Brownlee smoothed out his hair and plumped out the dents in his costume. Then with a straight face he started to do the Highland Fling around the living room. It was a dance he'd learned as a boy living in Scotland and whenever he did it, it sent his children into fits of giggles but it had double the impact with the giant pudding.

Tiger had only just regained composure and this was too much for him to bear. "No please stop, I can't take any more, Man! Please!" he lay on the floor laughing uncontrollably and this time everyone had to help *him* up and heave him onto the sofa. Mr Brownlee stopped dancing and let everyone catch their breath.

"Oh my goodness, you are insane," Polly panted.

"My stomach muscles are going to hurt tomorrow," said Tiger, clearly in pain.

Mr Brownlee kept his straight face and with a flick of his hair said, "If you'll excuse me, I am going to see how easy it is to visit the toilet. My underwear cost me £5 and I seem to have £3.50 of that wedged up my bottom."

Some time later, Mr Brownlee still hadn't emerged from the toilet and Polly sent Tiger to see what was happening. He did as he was asked and yet another roar of laughter went up as Tiger could be heard shouting, "He can't get out, he's stuck in the toilet doorway!"

Polly turned to Mrs Brownlee and said, "For a moment earlier I thought, what's that funny sound? And then I was like, oh yeah, it's my husband laughing. I've not heard it for so long you see, I'd quite forgotten what it sounded like."

"He's been such great value today, I can't imagine him being anything other than fun," Bea replied.

"Oh believe it," said TJ. "We've not even seen him smile properly let alone laugh for, well, years actually. Seriously, meeting you guys is the best thing that could've happened, isn't that right, Mum?"

Polly nodded pensively. "I don't think I've realised how miserable the two of us have been these past few months, it's totally changed over night. I just hope it stays this way."

"I'm sure it will," said Bertie with a smile. "He clearly adores you both."

TJ ruffled his floppy fringe, then held Bertie's gaze. "Thank you for being such an amazing friend. Best friend I've ever had in fact. You've done so much for me." Bertie felt a flush of blood to her face and shook her head in embarrassment.

Polly looked at her son with watery eyes. Then, she looked at Mrs Brownlee and took her hand.

"You do realise you're not going to get away from us now don't you?"

Mrs Brownlee chuckled. "I think we can live with that, don't you Bert?" Bertie smiled back. "Fine by me."

Just then the sound of acoustic guitars emanated from somewhere in the house. It grew closer and louder until all of a sudden the two dads reappeared in the doorway. Mr Brownlee was still in his Christmas pudding costume and Tiger was wearing a huge round Christmas bauble outfit with his rock star sunglasses.

"Ha ha ha haaaaa! I can't believe you brought that with you Brian," cackled Mrs Brownlee. "Tiger, it really suits you!"

TJ and Polly laughed hysterically.

"Oh my word, Dad! What are you wearing?"

"Look at that," said Bertie pointing at Tiger. "He can even make a ridiculous bauble costume look cool. I bet *he* could get up again if he rolled over and he'd do it with style, eh Dad."

Neither men cracked a smile and on the count of four, they launched into Mr Brownlee's song from the night before with Mr Brownlee doing his Tiger Jonz impression and Tiger doing an exaggerated version of himself, including his trade mark high leg kicks. Without hesitation, the women and children leapt to their feet and danced around the living room chanting:

> You and me (clap)
> She makes three (clap)
> He, she, you, me, family (clap)

When the song finished, they cheered each other and once again, flopped on the sofas to recover.

"Well that's worked off a bit of the turkey," puffed Mr Brownlee.

Bertie went over to give her dad a Christmas pudding hug. "Thank you for entertaining us."

Tiger removed his shades and mopped his sweaty brow. "Thanks for not taking any photos, you guys, it would surely end my career if anyone saw me in this."

He reached over to Mr Brownlee and slapped his back. "You write some great songs, Man."

"Me? Really?"

"Yeah Man, totally awesome. You've got skills."

Mr Brownlee laughed in disbelief. "You think *I've* got skill? Wow! That's some compliment coming from you."

"Don't laugh, I mean it, Man, you've written some mean tunes."

Mr Brownlee didn't know what to do with his face. It was so absurd to be praised by his idol and he wasn't sure how to handle it. Embarrassment and the desire to smile resulted in his facial muscles spasming into a sort of contorted toothy grimace. Luckily Tiger didn't notice; he was still in full flow.

"I've been in the studio trying to write stuff like that and nothing. Nada. Zilch. I just keep coming up with the same old stuff. I wanna write something new, something fresh, something that's gonna move people and get them fired up, like you can, you know?"

Mr Brownlee nodded enthusiastically but was totally stumped for words. This situation was so surreal – Tiger Jonz was telling him that he wished he could write songs like *his*. For a moment he wondered if he was having one of Bertie's mad daydreams and he finally understood how his daughter's mind worked.

Realising he hadn't spoken for a while, he found his mouth moving without that all-important filter.

"Well it's no wonder you haven't been able to write upbeat songs, look at the way you've been feeling lately. How can you write happy songs when you're feeling like poop?"

"Poop?" Tiger repeated.

"Poop," confirmed Mr Brownlee, his cheeks flushing scarlet. Did he really just say poop to an international pop star?

"So are you saying, if I scoop the poop, I'll be able to write better songs?"

"Would you like me to get you a pooper scooper?" was all that Mr Brownlee could think of in reply. Oh dear Lord. He wanted to put his head in his hands and weep.

Luckily Tiger threw his head back and laughed. He slapped Mr Brownlee on the back again.

"You give good advice *and* you've certainly helped to clear the poop. I've had a blast today, Man."

"Quick, go and write a song," quipped Mr Brownlee.

"Only if you write with me."

A shock of silence hit the room. Tiger stared expectantly at Mr Brownlee who stared back with his jaw somewhere near the floor.

"What? Me? Me? Don't be daft. I can't write songs like you can."

"No," said Tiger, "you write better ones. Can you get any time off from your job to help me write? Where do you work?" Mr Brownlee shook his head with his mouth still hanging open. It was a few seconds before he managed any words.

"As of yesterday, nowhere." He flicked his wife a wry smile.

"Great," said Tiger. "Then come and work with me."

CHAPTER 32

The day ended just as perfectly as it had begun; cold and snowy outside, dark and cosy inside with just the twinkle of fairy lights for that festive glow. The difference was, two families' lives were now complete, with all loose ends neatly tied.

Song writing. Of course. It seemed so obvious now. *That* was her dad's destiny – the talent that had been there all along - he just hadn't seen it, just like the white car. So he *had* got off that train in that awful dream after all. Mr Muse was a genius and if she could grow up to be half as good a Dream Dweller as he was, she would be a very happy girl.

Just before bed, at the end of the most perfect of days, Mrs Brownlee had one last surprise for her loved ones.

"I saved these so that it would make Christmas Day last that little bit longer."

She produced the exquisitely wrapped presents that Mr Muse had left under the tree when they had first arrived and handed them to their rightful recipients.

Each gift was, of course, perfectly picked. A silver harmonica for Billy to kick start his talent for music, a leather bound notebook and pen for Dad to write his new songs in, a gold necklace with a pendent of Morpheus for Mum. And for Bertie? She smiled to herself as she carefully unwrapped a pair of spectacularly sparkly black ballet pumps. Tucked inside one of the shoes was a little note, which read:

'To climb mountains in.'

The End

ACKNOWLEDGEMENTS

Starting to write a book is exciting but making it to the end is quite a feat. You need a purpose; something that drives you to keep the fire alive and for me it was my daughter, Tèa. Thank you for being you.

Huge thanks to Hope Jepson for the fabulous cover. I really appreciate all your hard work with such a short deadline! You did an amazing job.

Thanks must also go to Mark Taylor. Thank you for your words of wisdom, experience and advice and for giving up so much of your time to answer all of my annoying questions. You've been an amazing support and you made the whole publishing process so much easier!

Thank you to all my family and friends for their support, especially Natalie Ward – I really appreciate your enthusiasm throughout this journey, it's been so encouraging.

I also want to thank two people who unknowingly inspired me to create something that will live on long after I'm gone; Lisa Parker and Run Wrake. I may not leave a legacy as inspirational as yours but thank you for giving me the motivation to try.

Printed in Great Britain
by Amazon